HAN M GREENBARG

Elf Bat Book One: Kiah

Defend And Honor
The Fallen
For All Life Is Sacred
Their Memory Is Precious
And Their Value Is Worthy

May The Light Of Purity
Find Your Spirit
And May The Reckless Call
Of The Wild Blue
Bring You Home

— The Elf Bats Of Sidhovvn And The
Breath Of Their Creator,
Han M Greenbarg

Contents

Preface

Greetings, my friend. I welcome you into the realm of the Elf Bats, and I hope that you are enchanted with the characters in it. This is a story I have held with me since my early college years (I'm in my 30s now)...and I kept all these beloved characters in spiral notebooks until I felt ready to tackle it as a series. I cherish each of the Elf Bats that still live in my imagination, and every day, even as I write about different worlds and new characters, I hope that this story will find its way into your heart. I wish you the best in your life, your journey in whatever you are pursuing, and that you keep imagining beautiful things.

Not all nightmares stay forever. Eventually they will turn into dreams. It may take years before a struggle in your life has gone...but one day you will find and realize how important you are in this world. This story is for you to get lost in. A story to help you see other realms, other dreams, other possibilities. Fantasy has always helped me escape when I want to feel shielded from a fast-paced society. I hope it is a shield for you too.

Happy reading,

Han M Greenbarg

1

Banegildacht

KIAH

Discordant shrieks and clang of metal against rock woke him on a midnight winter solstice. The nightmares that stirred the little Bat prince before this night would never bear the same malice as the ones that came after.

"Mama?"

He followed the noise down the corridor and up the stairs to the war-training room of his parents. Bulky, hunched shadows moved around him in the cave; shadows of people who did not belong in a Bat home.

"I had a bad dream," he said to the figures in the room, shivering under the blanket he pulled over his head. He took three steps closer.

"Mama?"

Two hulking soldiers guarded the middle of the rock floor. There was a third being, a creature sunk on its knees with a blade pressed to its neck.

"Kiah," the less heavily armed of the two soldiers said.

Kiah tilted his head back to look up at him. The soldier knew his name. On closer look, this person wasn't a soldier at all, but a count from the court of the king. He wore thick rings on seven of his fingers and smelled of freesia, a scent of purebred royalty.

"Little prince," the count said in a harsh whisper as Kiah looked down at the creature on its knees.

The creature looked like a ravenous or diseased goblin-boar with matted, stringy hair and a bloody mouth, skin torn from its arms and torso.

"Kadhle, Kadhle," the count murmured to it.

In his sleepy haze, little Kiah couldn't understand the name.

"Refusing my warmth to the last." The count circled the creature. "Now your son comes to you. Your only child. He comes to die."

If not for the blade in the hand of the count, his voice would be a comfort in the dark room which bore shadows never conjured before. But Kiah was shaken, and in a closer look at the hair and dismantled garb of the creature, his legs buckled and he dropped to his knees. It was his mother.

"K'adhlenalde, Queen of the Bats, wife to Jekkiliah." The count's voice carried a chilling timbre as he circled them, iron blade scraping against the rock. "By order of the king, you must be sacrificed."

The purple streak in his mother's eyes pulsed lightly as she took shallow breaths. Her eyes met Kiah's from beneath the curtain of matted hair hanging over her face. No sound, no cry came from her broken jaw as she stared back at her child.

"I had a bad dream," Kiah said, crawling forward. Tears filled his eyes. "Mama?"

"Fractal," the count uttered.

The thick-bodied soldier holding the blade to K'adhlenalde's throat gave a terse jerk of the head to his master.

"Kill."

At the count's command, Fractal slashed the blade to one side and the Bat queen's body struck the cave floor. Kiah rocked back onto his rear, blanket slipping off his shoulders, small body wracked with tremors as he watched the soldier drag his mother toward the stairs. The soldier halted his step when he heard the count speak aggressively to the Bat child.

"Little prince," the count said. The forbidding cackles that came from his mouth pushed Kiah's tears to flow. Kiah shivered as he looked up at the king's servant.

"Do you know what I did to your father?"

At the little prince's silence, the count sunk to one knee, reaching to touch his pale, trembling face. The shivering child had eyes just like his mother except for a streak of ice blue striped beside the bright purple in each iris. Bat eyes held an entrancing spell of their own.

"He fought me with his sword as bravely as your mother. I stabbed him through the chest. No armor to pierce." The count glanced briefly toward the dead Bat queen's blood trail before looking back at the child. "All Bats must pay. But you, little prince, are no threat to the king." He unsheathed a knife from his hip and held it to Kiah's neck. "You will never have the strength to avenge Jekkiliah. I'd rather see you cry."

Grief overtook Kiah, his limbs convulsing as he tried to stand but fell back down onto the hard floor. The count stood up and barked an order at the soldier.

"Fractal, bring her."

"No...no, don't leave. Don't take my mama," Kiah sobbed between tearful breaths. His legs refused to pick him up. The moment the backs of the enemy were turned, dragging his mother's body with them, he smelt the smoke-kelp scent of his best friend's hair right behind him.

"I'm here, Bat. I'll look after you."

"Why, Spindle? Why have they come?"

Young Spindle, a half-elven pirate, embraced his friend as he wept. The cacophony of distressed Bat shrieks echoed in the cave's corridors as they held each other in the night.

"Death Order by the king," Spindle whispered. He whipped his head to the left, sensing shadows of new soldiers peering up the stairs. "Banegildacht."

2

Kiah

12 YEARS LATER

"There you are," Spindle said, poking a rod into the fire burning low beneath a pot of boiling brown sludge. The clink of his layered earring-chains dangling from both ears echoed in the cave, a familiar morning sound to Kiah.

The warmth of the hearth room circulated within a small part of the cave, flowing down the narrow corridor, past the forbidden upstairs. Spindle grinned as he poured some of the thick liquid into a shallow bowl and set it on the Bat's table.

"What's the smile for?" Kiah asked with a scowl. He approached with a weary hunch, his eight-foot frame towering over the half-elven. "You don't wake me this early, Spindle, and certainly you don't ever walk in here wearing those crusty boots."

"I made your breakfast. Hot mushroom stew and berries on the side just as you like."

Kiah squinted, tilting his head and biting his lower lip. "Where's the pudding? Lavender pudding is breakfast, stew is dinner."

"I'm leaving," Spindle said.

"Come now, cabin boy, where is my tea?" The Bat prince sat in his chair and leaned over the table to pick up raspberries one by one using only his teeth.

"Did you hear me, Hezekiah?"

"Yes, yes," Kiah said, berry juice dribbling from his top fangs as he positioned himself to dunk headfirst into the stew.

"I'm leaving," Spindle said again.

"No, you're my caretaker. What else have you to do?"

"My crew has a ship waiting for me on the northeast end of Sidhovvn. The opportunity I've spent my life waiting for has come and I shall not spare another day tending to a grown Bat prince who can care for himself."

Hearing the serious tone in his friend's voice, Kiah growled into the bowl and snapped back, rising quickly from the table as he did so.

"Spindle the pirate never makes such a terrible joke. You can't leave me now. I'm one month away from entering Coalhsomeii and I will be at my most vulnerable."

"There's time."

"Look at my claws. Look at my fangs. I can't hold a spoon or pour my own tea."

"You will make do, Bat," Spindle said, grey eyes rolling up to glance at the thick paste of animal bat feces stuck in the crevices above him. "You are a capable creature."

"My bottom fangs are still erupting, each joint in my arm aches from the growing claws, I walk only ten paces before needing to crawl like a wounded spider for stability."

Spindle watched with peeved amusement at Kiah's ranting and pacing before he finally took a seat, crossed one knee over the other, and settled in for an extended story about the Bat's growing pains. He drew a knife from the ratty pack on his shoulder and started to polish it with the sleeve of his coat.

"Swallow the tablet I gave you for the dizzy spells."

"Your pirate medicine has no healing power in my blood. Whatever powder you mix into it forces me to vomit."

"Ah." Spindle grinned slyly as he glanced up, locks of oily hair tangling in his left silver earring-chain. "That's the lucid agent at work."

"If I could only have one night without a bad dream," Kiah grumbled.

"Try laying on your pillow without your father's war helmet suffocating your head and his celibacy cloak stifling your veins. You should not be sleeping with any extra weight, nor should you carry that thing around under your arm like a child's luck charm."

Kiah looked down to what Spindle gestured at. "A feeble insult, Spindle. Someone didn't have his ale before waking me."

The Bat's natural speaking voice had the air of a gentle mountain brogue, each word coming out as if he had just spent the entire previous night weeping or shrieking hoarsely from nightmares. There were always nightmares. The evidence of an aging shadow never left his face.

"It is not a celibacy cloak. The white represents purity. He wore it on his wedding day to Mama. And this here," he said, lifting his father's eagle-shaped helmet with both hands, "is a part of my family. No more of Father's history will be taken when I wear it." He fit it on over his head, tucking his long, matted hair in under it.

"You look like an overgrown child playing with his grand-daddy's toys. Come, Kiah. Get out of that thing and take off the celibacy cloak."

"Purity!" Kiah screeched from inside the heavy helmet.

"For one, it doesn't go with the rest of your mourning attire, and for another..." Spindle trailed off, spending several minutes observing his friend standing in front of him. "How old was he when he married your mother?"

"Eighteen years."

"Same age as you are, Bat. Which if I understand Bat tradition correctly, you are teetering past your prime for a wife."

"Meaning?" Kiah sat back down, keeping the helmet on as he faced Spindle.

"That cloak is now a celibacy sign, not a purity one. You will never find a woman to put up with your sour mood."

"I can thrive without love."

"In the shadow of the cave, aye, but not out there." Spindle pointed with his knife to the cave's entrance, the ledge where the world fell away into the sunrise.

"Promise you will fly out one time to the top of the king's citadel."

"If they see, me I'm dead." Kiah slowly lifted the helmet up off his head, shook his hair, and combed through the knots with his claws. "You know I hate to fly."

"I've never seen you open your wings in all your growing up. You must trust they work."

"I won't fly without Mama to watch me."

Spindle rose from the table. "Then I guess you never will. At least climb down to do your pacing in the meadow. Don't let your face stay moonstone white forever."

"The sun has never been my solace. I'm retiring to sleep."

"Back to bed already? Why not paint me a farewell portrait?"

Kiah turned his back, dropping to a crawl halfway down the corridor when dizziness overtook him. Clutching the helmet tight, white cloak dragging along the rock floor, he crawled into his father's room.

"I will return for your hibernation," Spindle said. "I promise." He raised one arm above his head as he backed out of the cave. "Avenge Jekkiliah. Avenge your blood, Bat!" He pointed a finger to the sky as he prepared to climb down the cliff. "Let them see you fly."

Kiah curled up at the foot of the master bed, cloak wrapped around him. He considered trying to fall asleep upside down in the empty weapons closet, then hesitated as he remembered why he never bothered to put himself in that position. Father took his last breath that way.

He had no desire to see the world outside the cave, no desire to look upon the city of the killers. He only craved a sleep of peaceful dreams. If there could be one good dream to eradicate his mind's terror, it would make everything all right again. It would make him smile. A dream of Father's spoken tales of childhood mischief or Mama's voice singing the ethereal lullaby of Ialchagor.

He whimpered as he closed his eyes. Just one good dream. Before he knew fear. Before he knew death.

3

Daughter of a Count, Servant of a King

The king's court was the deepest sanctum within the citadel, a space in which business between Sidhovvns and foreign travelers occurred daily without a vocal quarrel or crossing of blades. Fly held her place on the marble floor at the harp, never breaking tune until the king's order to desist. Four of her working hours required sitting still with her instrument, the rest of her day lay out in the king's city taking inventory of each household's sustenance, on the streets where she had spent her childhood years seeking out the wild Elf Bats to prove King Averee wrong.

No breed of Elf dares to spill the blood of its kin without conscience, Fly thought, *save for the king himself.* Averee, purebred royalty, was more cruel than any bloodletting monster he told stories about. He could barely grip a standard sword, trembling as he tried. A curse of arthritis plagued his entire arm length, a curse which many commoners in Sidhovvn believed he brought onto himself in hopes of an easy rule over all living creatures.

"Fly, my child, don't be in such a rush."

"Yes, my liege."

"The harp is not made for rough-handling. Slow it down."

King Averee walked past Fly, gliding down the center of the court to the long table set several paces before his throne. He spent few hours in motion, preferring to sit within any of the fifteen sapphire-gilded seats in the room for an extended rest. His dark eyes, white hair, and gnarled hands gave him little pride among his servants, yet they still owed him their loyalty in exchange for a safe haven from Sidhovvn's underworld.

"My king Averee," called a voice. "I have new armor crafted for our soldiers."

Fly saw who approached in haste. It was Count Addis.

"Pleasant dawn, lass," the count said.

She faltered at his glance, her fingers slipping from the harp. At Averee's look of disgust for ruining his background muse, she dipped her head down and returned to the melody.

"Father," she said to the count. "Morning to you."

Addis nodded at her and continued forward to Averee. "We desire a gathering in the center of your city."

"Who is desiring this?"

"Myself and the eight other counts you've appointed for each village in Sidhovvn. A discussion must be raised about the recent letters from Ixetmori. The humans of the southern province are willfully answering her call for an army."

"She would not amass such a force against the city."

"My king," Addis said, "you must understand that Ixetmori is a threat."

Both the king and her father suddenly turned to stare at Fly. "Daughter," Addis said, "if Averee permits you to leave, I suggest you follow orders. Finish your day's work early and return home."

"Because of what my mother writes to us?" Fly asked with an innocent tilt of the head.

"Not a word, Butterfly. Leave the court."

At Averee's slow nod, she left her place at the harp and headed down the front hall, pausing when she heard her father speak in a fiery whisper behind her.

"My king, this is not a harmless trick. She was never meant to be a part of my household."

"Why in the name of grey Bat ashes did you marry her, Addis? You tell me now she has gone mad, when at the receiving of your daughter you were both the most joyous creatures in my court."

"Not anymore," Addis said. "There is nothing left of her heart."

Fly walked slowly, mulling their conversation, while at the same time thinking hard about what sacred object she had once planned to find and steal from the king. Her mental strength often distorted by false tales from the soldiers, and her lack of book education having left gaps in proper knowledge, she had grown to develop her own means of problem-solving. A means in which common sense was a final resort, and foolishness was always the answer.

"The book!" The sudden recollection stopped her in her tracks. An ancient book of the king. A cruel book she wanted to take and burn to cinders. "The Royal Methods of Elf Bat Torture," she whispered to herself. That was the title. She remembered it spoken from the king's lips.

Fly considered for a moment the free time she had on her hands, and the lack of empathy that King Averee had for creatures different from his own kind. *Justice*, she thought, *needs to be taken on this day.* She turned around, charging back into the court. The book was on the far corner of the long table. Purple leather binding, ragged, perhaps pages were missing. But it was there.

"Fly, bring that back! Butterfly!"

The angry voices echoed as she ran up the stairs, running as fast as she could onto each landing until she reached the citadel's top balcony. The entire floor was open to the air and looking about her surroundings, Fly realized there was one last maneuver to outwit the king. She peered over the edge of the smooth, white rail and secured the book in her pack strapped across her shoulder.

"Xavile!" she yelled to the horse grazing at the bottom of the tower. She swung one leg over the rail. "Stay, horse," she said, seeing him start to plod away from the wall of the citadel. "Ready to run!"

"Daughter, don't you jump!"

"Send the soldiers after her!"

She jumped, plunging down swift and hard onto Xavile's back.

To be a servant of nobility meant maintaining the appearance of a flawless face, tamed hair, and gracious etiquette in the purebred Elf society. The reckless streak in Fly's core had been forced to remain dormant during her formative years. Always desiring to be let free. To run wild.

"Go, Xavile. King's Cliff," Fly breathed into the horse's ears. She rode straight past the city's entrance torches, fully lit in the morning light, and glanced once more over her shoulder to see the king's soldiers coming behind her on foot. They were broad, bulky creatures who stood at eight feet tall but so thick with muscle one would not know they were part Elf.

"Arrows are coming," she said into the wind as they crossed the open meadow leading right to the steep cliff that peaked beyond the clouds. "Royal dirtmongers."

The arrow rain did not slow Fly as she urged Xavile to the base of the cliff and stood up on his back. She reached one arm up and gripped the rock, beginning the vertical climb. The harsh winter wind churned through her hair, loosening the braid, leaving her long red locks wild about her face. Loose rock wedged under her fingernails and trickled past her legs as she found her upward rhythm.

Fly was a lean purebred, typical for her age and bloodline, but she did not know her true origin. She only sought to do what felt right in her mind, what felt honest in her way of being. The arrows from the king's soldiers did not frighten her as she ascended the cliff, each one striking the solid rock around her in a careless arc. *If they wanted me dead, I would be fallen*, she thought. They knew how to aim. It was only a test to turn her back for home, to make her cry for her life. Death did not scare Fly, the daughter of a count, servant of a king. Death was an act of courage in her mind. A proper ending would be a beautiful thing for an imprisoned girl.

Then an arrow struck. Fly had one hand gripping tight to a ledge above her, and the other immediately pressed against her side. The warm, red wetness of her own blood. She suddenly couldn't feel any sensation in the fingers that held the ledge and started to slip.

"My dear," came a mellow voice from above her. It was an Elf Bat.

"Don't let me fall," she said, barely mouthing the words.

Within seconds of feeling the Bat grab her and pull her up onto the ledge, everything went dark.

4

Curiosity

Kiah picked up the Elf maiden's limp body, cradling her as he backed into the cave. The Bloodmanghe remained at the foot of the cliff armed with their bows. They were not light enough to scale the rock so quickly, but they would seek out the girl's protector and send word to the king. He laid her down on the single carpet in the hearth room, careful not to create a deeper wound from the arrow that was embedded in her body. The hour to save her was short.

An inner will of protection created a shiver in Kiah's wings, sending his entire body into a convulsion. He had near forgotten that he wore such power at his back. It pushed him into a vertical leap and lateral twist, shutting the cave entrance closed with the thrust from his wings. He heard his own breath loudly in the darkness, no flame burning on the hearth, every bit of power slipping until his wings dropped between the shoulder blades in a motion of defiant retirement. The Bloodmanghe could not get in and the girl could not get out.

She remained unconscious while Kiah prepared to pull the

arrow from her ribs. The only cry that came from her mouth was a low whimper when he closed up the gaping wound. Her eyes opened at midday as Kiah covered her shivering body with a thick blanket from his mother's closet. The maiden's eyes were pure ice. Sharp and wild. But she spoke soft, her vocal tone huskier than most purebred females.

"Soldiers," she mumbled.

"They've gone."

She looked like she was about to smile, then winced as she shifted under the blanket.

"The arrow went deep," Kiah told her. "Lay quiet."

She breathed out hard, curly red hair tangled around her face. "You're an Elf Bat."

Kiah stepped back, staring intensely at her. "Do you want to hurt me?"

"No," the maiden said. "No, I won't hurt you." She passed out again.

FLY

Fly opened her eyes to a dull pain in her torso and the sight of the Bat standing by the hearth, his back turned to her as he stirred up a fresh fire.

"You must come from warrior blood," he said. "You have a silent strength."

Fly opened her mouth to respond, then suddenly realized she was not wearing the same clothing she had been chased in. She pushed one edge of the blanket off her chest and tried to sit up.

"You're wearing a bodysuit of my mother's." The Bat turned around. "The blood soaked through your clothes."

Breathless and sore, Fly laid back down.

"I promise I did not dishonor you," the Bat continued. "My

people hold females in great purity."

She nodded, resigning herself to whatever fate came as she watched him stare at her with unblinking eyes.

"Are you going to hurt me?" he asked as he approached.

"No." Fly saw the distrust in his body language. "I said it before, Master Bat. I won't hurt you. Why don't you believe me?"

The Bat went to the lone, grey wood table in the middle of the room and picked up the pack Fly had carried with her. He pulled out the book from the king's court.

"This book," he said with a snarl. "Why do you have it?"

"I stole it from the king."

"Why?"

"I won't hurt you, Master Bat. I'm a friend." Fly pressed a hand to her side as she slowly sat up.

"You come from the citadel. Why do you carry this book?" The streaks of color in his eyes flickered as he stood over her, fangs prominent, his lower gums oozing blood.

"I took it from the king to destroy it. The Elf Bats are beautiful creatures to me. I promise, Master Bat," Fly said as she struggled to her feet. She noticed the tremendous height difference between them as she tilted her head back to look in his eyes. "I know the horrors that book holds and I despise it."

"You are not like the others?" he asked.

"I am not."

He held the book out to her and jerked his head to the fire. "Show me."

Fly took it from him and stood within an inch of the warm hearth, extending her arm above the flames.

"I respect your people," she said, her voice confident, and let the book fall, hearing its pages rustle as it began to burn.

The tension in his shoulders faded and he appeared to sigh in relief, but his expression remained dour. The Bat bowed his head and stepped back toward the table, placing two wooden bowls filled with brightly colored sustenance on its surface. Fly hadn't seen where the food or dishes had come from and blinked hard at the perplexing illusion.

"Are you hungry?"

She nodded, and at the gesture of his arm, sat down in one of the chairs.

The Elf Bat had no beard, yet his pale skin looked rough, worn from age. His eyes were empty of spirit, containing no lively spark, as if his entire childhood had been made through a weary animal's survival mode. Yet they were still beautiful. The colors were just as transfixing as she had imagined a Bat's eyes would be.

"It's the eyes, right? No one can get past that." His voice sounded gentler now, a strong mountain creature's accent with a raspy undertone.

"Your eyes are blue like mine," Fly said.

"My eyes are not yours." He sounded offended as he raised the bowl to his lips. "You don't see the other color?"

"Yes, Master Bat. I heard about the multicolored irises in Bats. The colors are always passed down the bloodline."

The Bat clumsily set the bowl down, claws at the ends of his hands scrabbling against the table. He wiped one arm across his mouth, dirtying the sleeve of his black tunic.

"You claim knowledge of my people," he said.

"I've heard many stories of the Bats. I never imagined that I would meet one in my lifetime." Fly watched him sit perfectly still across from her. "Can you tell me your name?"

He hesitated before answering her, lowering his head until

his dull, stringy hair covered his face. "Kiah."

"I'm Fly."

KIAH

The mirth in the maiden's eyes favored her youth, untouched by death's torment. There was something endearing about her naïveté, and meek but restless spirit.

"Fly? What sort of people gave you that name?"

"I was given the name Butterfly," she said. "But I don't know who chose my name. I was adopted as a baby."

"You don't know your origin?"

"No, Master Bat."

Kiah glanced at the bowl of lavender pudding in front of Fly. She still hadn't touched it. "You must come from warrior blood. As I said before, my dear, you are very strong."

He had removed the white cloak and war helmet right before the rescue, placing them back in his father's room. Fly seemed trustworthy, but Kiah didn't want her to survey the possessions of his family without his permission.

"Pain leads to good things. My father told me that," she said. "Although I am not sure I believe him."

"Your father?"

"Not my real father. The couple who raised me are a purebred male Elf and his wife of human kin."

"You don't know where you come from," he stated.

"No."

"Knowledge of one's history is important, Fly." He paused long after speaking her name, pondering the sound of the letters, the meaning and connection to the maiden's adoptive family and true blood relations, wherever they might be. "Fly," he said again.

She smiled at him, a timid smile. He didn't smile back. He knew that he looked like an ugly, haggard beast.

"You do not wish to see me dead, my dear?" he asked her.

Fly hovered over the bowl of pudding, the ends of her red curls raking across the top of the milky purple substance. She still wasn't lifting it to her mouth. She just stared at it, studying it closely.

"I was taught to fear the Bats, but I chose not to listen. I think how I wish to think," she finally said, her attention going back to her bowl as soon as she was finished speaking.

"You truly are a different one then," Kiah said.

She laid a hand on the table's surface, moving her fingers forward to grip the bottom of the bowl. She continued to speak without looking up at Kiah. "The king has no right to wish you dead, Master Bat."

"That is kind of you. Your pudding is getting cold."

Fly looked up at him quizzically then back to her bowl, pursing her lips. "It's meant to be eaten hot?"

"Aye." Kiah tilted his bowl forward to show her how much he had consumed. "I make it myself."

"The color is not a usual thing."

"Lavender pudding. It may be a strong taste for you."

As Fly picked up the bowl with both hands and brought it to her lips, Kiah thought about the way in which she tried to show respect to his people. He had not anticipated such deep admiration from a purebred. No fear, no wrath in her gentle, wide-eyed face. There was an endless childlike curiosity in Fly, a desire to learn of a life beyond her own haven, and yet, she was a fragile woman who still needed protecting herself.

"May I have more, Master Bat?"

She thrust the bowl out to him after tilting it back and gulping all of it down with the same vigor as Spindle had attacked a stash of ale. The exuberance, the mess, the wild expression on Fly's face nearly cheered Kiah's heart.

"You eat like an animal," he said, looking from the pudding in her hair to the purple splatters on the table.

Fly pointed at him and then at his bowl. "Wild mirrors wild, doesn't it? I'm not like the other purebreds."

Kiah nodded as he picked up their bowls to refill them at the pot above the hearth.

"Indeed not," he whispered. "You are reckless."

"I hear that as a compliment, Master Bat," she smiled.

"Call me Kiah." He started to move back to the table, halting in his tracks as he felt his legs weaken.

"What's wrong?"

"Forgive me. My body tires fast."

"Let me," Fly said in a hastened voice, rising from her chair. She stepped quickly to reach him as he staggered, his entire eight-foot height careening over the maiden's short frame. "I got you." She allowed herself to be used as a crutch, getting them both back to the table.

Kiah breathed a sigh as he set the bowls down. Not a drop of his favorite sustenance had spilled. Of all the things he consumed at his table, lavender pudding was the one he least liked to waste. The taste of it reminded him of the joyous home that used to fill the cave. He recalled the comfort of a warm bowl before him as he and Mama giggled at Father's wild stories by the light of the hearth.

"Master Bat?"

He squinted at Fly, his vision blurred, as she seemed to be smiling at him like an eager child.

"My dear," he acknowledged. He tried not to show his

physical discomfort as he began eating his second helping.

"How tall are you? I was trying to figure it out as I stood beside you, and I know I am quite short in comparison. I'm near six feet. A typical purebred height I was told."

"I am eight feet tall."

"Are you a full-grown Elf Bat?"

"In height yes, but in other ways…" Kiah glanced down at his claws, felt the pain in his throbbing gums, tried to shake away the blurred, double vision. "I will not be fully-fledged for another month."

"What does that mean?"

"It means I will have a great physical strength that I do not carry now."

"Are you not strong for your age?"

"All Bats suffer in their transformation."

Fly looked long at his weary face as she set her bowl down. "How old are you, Master?"

"Eighteen years."

"You don't look it."

"Death ages you, my dear. I've seen lots of it."

"I'm eighteen too. Perhaps I look more like a child than a grown female Elf."

Kiah nodded at her. "Indeed."

<u>FLY</u>

"If I may ask, what happened to your parents?" she asked him.

"Dead."

"Both of them?"

"Aye."

"Are you the last Elf Bat in Sidhovvn?"

He didn't answer.

"Master?"

"Call me Kiah."

"The king said that an army of humans killed off the Bats years ago. Is that what became of your mother and father?"

"Mama and Father died in a lightning storm."

"Lightning?" Fly covered her amused smile with a hand. "Who dies in lightning?"

"I don't like storms. I never go out in the rain."

"Are you afraid of lightning, Master Bat?"

Kiah eyed her with furrowed brows. "You can call me Kiah, my dear."

"But you deserve more respect than that. Do you know how special you are in this country?"

"I am the last of my kind. That is all, Fly."

"What else are you? Did you see the war that the king spoke of?"

Kiah stood up and leaned over the table. "You ask so many questions."

"I want to know."

"Yet you already seem full of knowledge, Fly, servant of the king. What do you know of Bat culture?"

"I..." Fly found herself startled by the intensity in his eyes, the enchanting streaks of blue and purple. "Only what my father told me."

Kiah stepped backward, sternly looking down at her as she remained in her chair. "So you know nothing."

"Forgive me, Master," Fly said, pressing a hand to her ribs. "One doesn't have to read a hundred books to learn a people's culture."

"I disagree, my dear. Books are crucial to understanding

history. If you can't read them then why bother asking the question at all..." his voice trailed off and Fly quickly looked away from him as her face reddened. "You can't read," Kiah said.

"They took books away from me when I tried to teach myself. I only know what the evil book said because I heard the king read it aloud every day."

"Why would they discourage you to learn? Did the king fear you would become wiser than him?"

Fly shrugged, face still hot with shame.

"Come," Kiah said. He extended his right arm to her. "I can teach you."

5

Bat Culture

Fly followed him down a corridor of the cave, noting the increased darkness and cold temperature as they walked through a rounded archway. The inside of the room was barely tall enough for Kiah to stand at his full height, and its width was only six inches wider than the two of them standing side by side. Books spilled out from the cracked frame of a low shelf in the corner, next to a table that held a single flickering candle. The bat excrement-covered walls and ceiling were layered with faded painted pictures that looked like the art of an enraged child.

"Did you paint these?"

"Aye," Kiah answered, squatting down to pick out a book from the shelf. "What city do you come from?" he asked as he stood back up.

A look of confusion came over Fly's face. "King's City. It is, is it not?"

Kiah placed the book onto the table. "No." He rifled through the pages of the thick volume and laid it open flat for her to see the text. "Adreachterum."

"What?"

"The proper name for Sidhovvn's main city is Adreachterum. This is one word of the ancient Bat language, or what is left of it."

"Ah-drach...?" Fly tried.

Kiah shook his head and pointed to the word on the page. "It is all right here, my dear. The proper way to pronounce it is written next to the word itself. Go on. Sound it out slowly."

"Ah-drahk-tear-em," Fly said, following each printed syllable. She looked back at his face as he leaned in over her shoulder.

"Good," he said. "Sit, my dear. Sit and I will show you."

As Fly sat at the table, she smelled a strong mix of cedar, teak wood, and ash. *Kiah's scent*, she thought. It was a pleasant guise against the animal stink of the Bat's unwashed hair and body. But Fly did not judge her rescuer's position. She was in awe of him. Never had she imagined she would be in the company of an Elf Bat, much less in his own home.

"Adreachterum is the largest in perimeter and population."

He turned the page with a tender touch, his left wrist brushing against hers as he guided her in reading the pronunciations of each word. His voice sounded poetic, soothing in the dim candlelight of the room. Fly wanted to listen to him for hours, in his teaching and sharing of ancient Bat text.

"These are all the names of the outer villages spread through Sidhovvn. Each of them is run by a separate count."

"I know that," Fly said.

"Do you know their names?"

"I only know my father's name."

Kiah's claw suddenly tore into the center of the page. "Your father is a count?"

"My adoptive father, yes. His name is Addis." Fly turned

her head to look back at him as he drew in trembling breaths. "What's wrong?"

"I'm all right, Fly." He let out a shaky breath and pointed back to the page. "Read the next name and the count who heads it."

He lightly ran his claw beneath the letters for her to follow.

"Flah-see-drome," Fly read.

"Floseadrom, aye. In the Bat language it means 'flower light'."

"Count Eed-mine?"

"Good, my dear. Eadmeihn. Remember, there is proper pronunciation and common pronunciation."

Fly turned her head to see his face right beside hers. She breathed softly as she felt his claws grip her shoulders. "Which is this?"

"Of course it is proper."

Kiah read through the name of each village and its designated count, gently prompting Fly in the proper pronunciation. Every name was laid out clearly in the book. The text appeared to be meant for teaching the young and ill-informed.

Village: Ireaachgr [err-ah-kah-ger]
  Meaning: "Weave Forward"
  Count: Deoraheii [dee-ohr-ah-ee-ay]

Village: Cinatbreidh [sin-at-breeth]
  Meaning: "Born in Ashes"
  Count: Adheatim [ath-ee-tim]

Village: Igneactta [ig-neek-tah]
  Meaning: "Fire Snow"

Count: Ignitehd [ig-nite-ed]

Village: Illarandu [ill-ar-ahn-doo]
  Meaning: "Spider in Leaves"
  Count: Uvleorm [oov-lee-ohrm]

Village: Raihatiac [rye-ah-tee-ahk]
  Meaning: "Gracious War"
  Count: Llieghonu [lee-eh-gohn-oo]

Village: Iragaodh [eer-ah-gai-oth]
  Meaning: "Wretched Wind"
  Count: Iratsuad [er-aht-soo-ad]

Village: Geisperadh [gai-spair-ath]
  Meaning: "Winter's Eve"
  Count: Fiieguin [fye-ee-goo-inn]

"Every word we speak now is what Bats call 'descendant language'."

"Did you speak Bat with your mother?"

"No. I did not." Kiah's response was somber as Fly flipped the next page and read the single word written on it.

"Eel-kah-gor."

"That's right. Ialchagor's Cliff. This cliff you climbed."

"It's called King's Cliff," Fly said with absolute confidence.

"No. Ialchagor."

"Who is Ialchagor?"

"It is not a person." Kiah seemed agitated. "It is an ancient Bat lullaby. A haunting, beautiful song that only a mother could sing to her child."

"Did your mother sing it to you?"

"I don't remember it. And I care not to go looking for the words." Kiah forcefully closed the book and yanked it off the table. He clutched it to his chest, giving Fly a pained look.

"Is it written somewhere in these books? Can't I learn the lullaby?"

"No, Fly. You cannot. Please refrain from speaking again of Ialchagor."

His stern voice echoed in the room and silenced Fly. She realized she had gone too far in her curiosity of her host. *Everyone has secrets*, she thought.

"I'm sorry." She stood, eyes downcast. The room felt even smaller in that moment. Their bodies lightly touched in the darkness as the candle burned itself out.

"There's so much I want to know about your people, but I do not mean to offend," Fly continued. "I never meant to intrude your sanctum."

The only response she received was the soft breathing of the Bat.

"You didn't have to save me," Fly whispered into the silence.

Kiah cupped her chin with both of his claws and lifted her head to look into his eyes. "In Bat culture it is the purpose of the males to protect and honor the females. It is the same reason I did not violate your innocence when I dressed you in my mother's clothing. I honor you as it should be for all."

Fly smiled, moving her hand up to touch his left claw. "Thank you."

"It is only right," Kiah said. "A male with such ill intent should never be blessed with the company of a female. He should bear honor for her, no matter his creed." He moved his claws to Fly's hair, running them down through the long curls. "If a male of any species cannot vow to protect his female, how can he live for anything but himself?"

Kiah still had not smiled at her, but the timbre of his voice was calming and gentle. "You are beyond kind, Master Bat. You are regal," Fly said.

"I am nothing of the sort. I fear more in this world than you can imagine."

"But it did not stop you from saving me. You could have let me fall."

Kiah drew closer, head bowed, mouth inches from Fly's, and she saw his fangs glimmer in the dark. "You told me to hold on. I would never let you go."

"Thank you," Fly said. She looked over her shoulder at the doorway. "Can we go back to the fire? I'm cold."

"Aye. Come."

Kiah led her back to the hearth room and helped her down onto the floor. He tucked a blanket around her. "I'd offer you another room in my cave to sleep, but this is the warmest. You need your rest, my dear."

Fly smiled, ready to hear more about the Bats. "How many rooms are there in here?"

"Six rooms down that corridor. I can show you the rest of it tomorrow if you desire."

"Where will you be?" Fly looked concerned as Kiah backed away from her makeshift bed.

"The room of my father. Rest, Fly."

"Goodnight, Master Bat," Fly said to herself as he vanished in the dark of the cave. Several hours passed before she could close her eyes. So much had happened in one day. So much had changed. She didn't want to leave the Bat. She wanted to learn everything about him.

6

The Garden of Magic Water

Kiah stood over Fly as she slept, head tilted, curious at how soundly the maiden snored. The sounds from her nose and mouth were loud for a female.

"It's well past sunrise," he said, watching her stir under the blanket. "Here's breakfast."

Fly opened her eyes and stared up at him. She looked troubled, like she had just awoken from a bad dream. "What's that?"

"More pudding." Kiah held the bowl out to her. "I added blueberries on top."

"Thank you." Fly sounded perplexed as she answered him. She sat up and took the lavender pudding. "I'm sorry, I don't usually eat sweet things in the morning."

Kiah almost smirked as he watched her tilt the bowl back and scarf it down. She didn't look sorry about eating his sweet pudding. She looked like she was ready to devour another bowl.

"Do you have tea?" Fly asked.

"Ingredients for it, aye."

"And more pudding?"

"Aye. You eat a lot for a female."

"Yes." Fly winced as she got to her feet.

"Still sore," Kiah noticed.

"A lot better. May I ask, Master Bat, where do you get all the ingredients needed for pudding and berries and tea?"

The maiden had proven to be harmless in the night, remaining in the hearth room and resting as she should. Her many questions sprouted from a meek and childlike heart. For the first time since the night of the Death Order, Kiah was beginning to believe that he could trust a purebred Elf.

"I have a garden," he said. "Come, let me show you around."

Fly walked alongside him as they moved down the corridor and past the book room. As he passed the stairway to their right, Kiah looked back to see that Fly had come to a halt.

"What is up there?"

"Nothing of note. Follow me."

She listened, keeping pace as she gave a curious glance to each room that they passed.

"I showed you my book room. The rest of the rooms down this corridor have served their purpose in the past as a Bat nursery, painting room, music room, and weapons storage. This room at the end here is my father's room."

They stood just outside the doorway, Fly's eyes moving from one object to the next. "You sleep here?"

"Aye. It's where I'm most comfortable and feel most safe."

"And the garden?" She tilted her head back to look in his eyes. "Where is it?"

Kiah wordlessly pointed straight ahead. The back of the cave did not end with a wall, but a ledge surrounded by a great mist and the sound of rushing water.

"Look down, my dear."

<u>FLY</u>

They were standing behind a waterfall. It dropped down into a pool that quickly narrowed into a crystal blue stream flowing out through a tiny gap in the rock. On the sides of the stream lay grass, flowers, trees, and all varieties of fruit. The only light inside the underground garden came from torches placed near the ceiling of the cave. Flowers that should not bloom without sun were thriving, and even in the damp, misty atmosphere sprouted plants that could only exist in a desert.

"How can so many species of flower and tree live together without sunlight?"

"The water," Kiah said in a soft voice. "It is magic."

"What power do you have to create that magic, Master Bat?"

"Magic is not power. It is not the answer to life or peace. It just is. It is a force we cannot understand, and no Bat tries to make sense of it. It just is, my dear. In the water, flowing everywhere, through every cave, every forest, every cliff, every valley, the water holds its own meaning."

"What is that?"

"Water is life," Kiah said.

Fly smiled and held out her arms, stepping forward to feel the rush of water. "Can I go down there?"

"Aye. There are steps to your left."

"So many ingredients to choose from!" Fly called out gleefully as she made her way to the grass. "May I make tea for us?"

"I should not have to ask you to do that, Fly. You are my guest."

"But your claws look quite ungainly and painful. Isn't it hard to make tea for yourself?"

"Aye."

Fly touched each plant, glancing up every so often to see if Kiah was watching her. "Aren't you coming down?"

"No. Go on and gather the ingredients."

"Do you ever swim in it?" Fly pointed to the pool beneath the waterfall.

"Not often, my dear."

"It's so beautiful. I could live down here."

"Come, Fly," Kiah said. "Orange, mint, green, strawberry, lemon, bottlebrush. Pick your tea."

Fly gave him a playful smile and bounded like a baby lamb into the pool.

KIAH

Watching from the top of the ledge, Kiah found himself smitten by Fly's childlike spirit. The joyous energy she embodied was unlike any creature he had heard of or seen with his own eyes. For a brief moment, Kiah wore a hint of a smile, imagining how his parents would have loved to act lively and foolish with Fly. But thinking of Mama drained the joy from his face. The memory of her last shrieks never left his mind.

"You are glistening enough from the water," he called out to Fly. "I will cook our dinner." He began the slow walk down to the grass, his dark cloak dragging along the wet rock.

"Master, I can do it." Fly ceased her splashing and stood straight in the pool. Her curls stuck to her face and soaked clothing. "I can pay you back."

"You do not owe me."

"You saved my life, Master Bat."

Kiah sighed as he turned his back to her. "Why do you not call me by name?"

"Certainly you deserve more respect from all of the purebreds in that city. You are not a monster. You are not what they say you are."

Fly's voice was quivering as she spoke, and when Kiah turned back around, he saw that she had stepped out of the water and stood only inches from him.

"I do not require payment, my dear Fly. You are free to return home without a debt to me."

"I want to learn more about your people." Fly shivered as she stared up into his eyes. "I want to learn about you."

Kiah took a step back. He considered the maiden's words and thought of every possible meaning she could have in her mind. "Do you wish to stay in my cave?"

"If I am given permission," Fly said. She appeared nervous, backing away toward the water. "I feel more at home now than I've ever felt anywhere."

"The eyes of a creature always reveal their life story. You can be a child of five years and have the darkest, soulless stare, and in the same room there can stand a being of two hundred years with the vigor and whimsical spark of a newborn. You are as intriguing as they come," Kiah said. He followed her to the edge of the grass. "I would be honored to have you stay."

Fly's smile warmed him as he rested the back of his right claw on her cheek. Her soft skin was as pale as his own, her eyes the same brightness as an innocent child's. "Butterfly, servant of the king, will you be my caretaker?"

"Yes."

"Then come, my little pudding. We can make tea together."

"What did you call me?" Fly asked.

Kiah found himself chuckling for the first time in years. The questions, the banter, the meek spirit that Fly embodied chased his sorrows out of the cave. "Little pudding," he repeated. "I thought such a pet name is fitting since you eat so much of it."

"Fair. A compliment to your cooking," Fly grinned. "Tell me, Master Bat," she said, as she trailed behind him, "why don't the purebred Elves think of you the way I do? You're magnificent, Kiah," she said, uttering his name firmly.

"Hezekiah."

"What?"

"My given name is Hezekiah," Kiah said, looking down at her.

"Do you have the legendary wings, Hezekiah?" Fly asked excitedly. "Wings as big and strong as a dragon's? Wings that can stir up great winds and firestorms?"

"I have wings, aye. But I do not fly."

"Why not?" she asked.

"I can't."

7

The Cliff

<u>FLY</u>

After preparing a meal together with the ingredients they had brought back from the garden, Fly changed into fresh clothing, another bodysuit of Kiah's mother's, the color a limestone pink. Kiah had also changed but donned the same black color as earlier.

"All Elf Bats can fly. Any animal born with wings knows how to use them. Shouldn't it be instinct?"

"I fear my wings cannot hold me."

"They must. They are a part of you." Fly took a handful of mushrooms from the table and tossed them into the boiling water. "Is it true that you can turn into an actual bat?"

"That is a myth from the king. He believes he knows my culture as well as his own, but there is no truth to his stories."

Out of respect for Kiah, Fly kept silent for a few moments, making eye contact with him as he thickened the stew over the fire. The manner in which he carried himself was timid and sorrowful, but he held a warrior spirit beneath his hunched, pained body. Fly still believed in the legends. She believed he had the wings of a dragon's power and that he could fly with an arrow's precision.

"What are you thinking of me, little pudding?" he asked in his gentle mountain brogue.

"May I see your wings?"

Kiah turned his back to her.

"May I see them, Kiah?"

"I cannot fly for you," he said.

"I just want to see. Please."

"Aye." The word came out hoarse. Kiah stepped away from the hearth and walked toward the corridor. "Come."

Fly followed, hesitating at the threshold of the Bat's sleeping quarters. "Am I allowed?"

He motioned her forward. "Aye. My father's room contains many relics of the family history, so do as I say, and leave each object as it be. You may watch me at the mirror."

Kiah stood tall in front of a full-length mirror, his reflection distorted by the grime and bat feces smeared across the surface. He could see Fly behind him and felt the intensity of her gaze as he shrugged off his dark cloak and tunic.

"You do have wings," Fly whispered.

"Aye." Kiah humbly lowered his head, avoiding his reflection. "It is not a piece of beauty, but a burden on my life."

"Tell me why you fear to fly."

"I will fall."

"You could not fall with these wings. They are glorious." Fly held her hand out to touch the ends of his wings. They were leathery, both cold as a reptile and warm as a bat.

"I would open them for you, pudding, but this room is not large enough for me to stretch out."

"Are they strong as a dragon, Kiah?"

"Some would say yes. I do not know what power mine hold."

"Can you spread your wings whilst wearing a cloak?"

"Aye. Most of my clothing is customized for the wings to settle against my back. They grew out from between my shoulder blades and now they lay against my skin as they are meant to. Some tunics are meant to contain them and not let the wings have freedom, but in a time of war, all Bats fly while wearing full armor and are still able to fully utilize the power of their wings."

"So you do know they are powerful."

"I know what they are capable of in a full-fledged Bat. I am not yet at peak strength."

Fly's admiration for Kiah overwhelmed her as she looked at herself next to him in the mirror. She knew he suffered from constant pain as his fangs were breaking through, but he showed his agony in silence. The kindness he imbued despite grief over the loss of his people in a senseless war was beyond respectable.

"Did your parents try to teach you to fly?" she asked.

"There is so much you have yet to know of me," Kiah said. "Of what I have endured. I need nourishment before any other action is taken at your beckoning. You are so curious, so wondering." He put his tunic and cloak back on. "Come."

KIAH

Kiah tasted the mushroom stew he had just served himself and Fly and quietly spat it back into the bowl. It was not as good as how Spindle made it. He watched Fly copy his method of slurping, tilting her bowl in her hands. She didn't appear disgusted with the meal placed before her, swallowing it down with startling velocity. Her enthusiasm made him smile and he tried to hide his amusement by clumsily lifting the bowl to his mouth.

"What did your mother look like?" Fly asked.

"She was of superior beauty."

"What makes a female Elf Bat superior?"

Kiah closed his eyes and set the awful stew down. "Too many qualities to explain, Fly. One could say the enchanting eyes, iridescent set of fangs, or the keen muscles in the legs. Female Bats are far more precious than males."

"And your father? Do you look a lot like him?"

"I hardly remember much of his face."

Fly giggled. "You were a mama's boy."

"Aye. You could say that."

"What else about your mother? What did she teach you?"

"She was supposed to take me up for my courage dive." Kiah fought the welling emotion as he left his chair and turned away. "She didn't live long enough."

"Kiah?"

"The courage dive," Kiah explained, his voice husky, "is meant for a mother and her child. It is a rite of passage for all Bat children."

"What age?" Fly asked.

"Usually we are seven years when we do it." He turned around, eyes glistening with tears. "You jump from the mother Bat's back and let yourself fall into the wind, opening your wings on instinct. Once you land on the ground, you get a sapphire ring for the accomplishment. We call it a courage ring. I would have kept my parents' rings but I lost them after they were killed."

"By lightning."

"Aye." Kiah remained stiff as Fly leaned herself against him. He felt her arms wrap around his body and he hesitated before circling his claws around her. Her hair smelled like lavender and musk. He breathed in deep. "Lightning."

<u>FLY</u>

"Can we watch the sky on the top of the cliff? I miss the natural light."

"It is a mile up. Do you not fear heights?"

Fly smiled up at Kiah, backing out of the embrace. "I love standing in high places and feeling the wind. It makes me feel alive."

"Indeed, you are a reckless one," Kiah sighed. "Let's go."

The journey up the steep Ialchagor's Cliff meant clinging to the tiniest of nooks in the rock just beyond the cave entrance. Fly felt right at home scaling it as she had done so before in a shower of arrows. She noticed Kiah next to her, pressed flat against the rock, managing to climb steadily with his long claws. His cloak whipped about in the winter chill as he surpassed Fly to the top.

"Everything is visible from this point," he said. "We stand higher than the roof of your king's citadel."

"A storm is coming," Fly said. "Clouds gather."

"Aye." Kiah backed away from the edge.

"Do you imagine leaping from here?"

"No. I do not."

"There is nothing to fear, Kiah." Fly twirled around, her arms in the air. "Just do what is natural for your kind."

"Do what?"

"Stretch your wings out. Dance with me."

Kiah shook his head as he watched her. "I do not frolic in such a manner, pudding."

"Would you catch me?"

"Catch you?" he repeated.

Fly took a step backward and her cheerful smile morphed into an intense stare. "Aye," she mimicked Kiah. Her curls flew across her face as she leaned back. "Catch me." She disappeared over the edge.

KIAH

"Fly!"

In the second that she was gone, fear escaped his mind, and courage opened his wings. He dove off the ledge, releasing a primal shriek into the wind. The colors in his Bat eyes pulsed as he chased Fly's falling body, this beautiful, curious, reckless female. There was no thought, no question in his head as he let his wings propel him down. Animal instinct and the voice of Mama echoing in his head overshadowed everything in his line of sight and sound. A perfect form, a perfect dive, in the moment of catching his Butterfly.

He grabbed her only inches from the ground, shooting right back up into the sky.

"You're flying, Kiah!"

He said nothing but smiled wider than he had in his entire life. They both started laughing.

"I knew you'd catch me," Fly said.

"You foolish girl," Kiah said, his voice glowing, joyful even.

"Your wings are magnificent. Seeing the world this way is the most magical thing I've ever experienced."

Kiah suddenly felt an urge to fly wilder, faster. "I have to put you down, pudding. I need to try something." He quickly brought her back to the cliff's edge and lunged over the side again, flipping and rolling in the air. The freedom of his wings unlocked every stalled part of his mind and heart. He flew in the way of his ancestors and in the way of Mama. The world would never look the same.

8

Bonding

<u>FLY</u>

"Have you always liked jumping from high places?"

"The intent was for you to fly, Kiah. I wouldn't risk my life like that for just anyone."

"You didn't need to act in such a manner." Strawberry juice dribbled from Kiah's fangs as he spoke. "You could have just pushed me."

Fly saw a smile on his face when she looked up at him from her own bowl of berries.

"Pushed you? And what would that have done?"

"To the same effect, pudding. You push me, I step out of the way, and my wings propel me to catch you as you tumble off the edge."

"That sounds like taking my life, not protecting it."

Kiah chuckled. "Just testing my reflexes, are you?"

Fly grinned back. "You're different when your wings are open. Playful."

"I can say I didn't know what I was missing, but it would have been nice to have a fellow Bat watch me take flight for the first time."

"I'm happy I saw it." Fly started to reach for a berry, then instead lowered her head as Kiah had, grabbing one out with her teeth.

"You're getting good at that," Kiah said. "You must be used to many rules back home. No space for acting like an animal."

"You're much better looking than an animal, Kiah."

"Did you know," he said to her, "that I don't like heights?"

Fly squished a blueberry in her front teeth. "But you just flew off a cliff."

"Instinct doesn't eradicate caution."

"It does. You caught me inches from the ground."

"You are the reckless one, pudding. I listened to my senses."

As Kiah held another strawberry in his fangs, Fly's expression changed, her eyes piercing his from across the table. "So did I."

KIAH

"Can you teach me how to paint?" Fly asked.

Kiah blew into the hearth, stirring up the flame. "There is no complexity in making art. Why must you ask me to teach you?"

"The paintings that you did. The ones in the book room. Can you show me how to do that?"

"Have you never painted on your own? Those were creations from my childhood. Nothing of great beauty."

"I couldn't help but notice the colors, Kiah. Why did you stop bringing bright colors into your home? Was it because of the war?"

Kiah straightened, sighing long as he faced Fly. "When my parents were alive, we used to dress in light blues and greens and golds of all hue. There was once color in this cave, aye. I still paint, but the moments are rare when I do."

"Will you show me?"

The joy in Fly's eyes urged Kiah to give a reluctant nod and he waved his arm for her to follow. The painting room was of a larger height and width, with a white fabric covering the whole of the rock floor. Kiah chose a brush from the left wall shelf and held it in his fangs as he dropped to his knees. He dipped it into a bucket of dark blue paint set to one side of the room and lifted his head to look at Fly.

"Watch me," he said between gritted fangs.

Kiah shook his head like a raging wolf, flinging paint from the brush in all directions. Blue paint streaked his brown hair and dripped down the sleeves of his tunic and leggings. Fly backed up to the far wall, shielding her face from the splatter.

"Are you," Fly asked, keeping her distance, "always this messy in your painting?"

Kiah let the brush fall out of his mouth and sat back on his heels. "Try delicately holding a thin brush with these claws, Fly. You won't get far."

"But must it be so violent?"

"You were certainly quick to imitate my messy eating. Why is painting any different?"

"Creating art is not the same as consuming food."

"You said it yourself, Fly." Kiah shifted to one knee. "You are not like the other purebreds."

"Well, yes. But I was taught that art and music are pleasures to be taken seriously. Done with method, precision."

Kiah smirked and spread his arms. "One does not need precision to make beauty. Come. It's your turn."

Fly stood with her back against the wall, head tilted as she stared at him. She looked to be in deep thought. Too much thought, and too little joy.

"Where has my little reckless butterfly gone?" Kiah said. "You were quick to fall backward off the cliff, and now, in the calmest of places, you hesitate? What makes you behave this way?" He stood up.

"I once sat in the court of a king, wearing a servant's dress and my hair tied back in a horribly boring fashion." Fly backed away as Kiah followed her. "I once played the harp for six hours to please the king and still he insulted my blood. Children in the city streets mocked me. They called me the daughter of goblin-boars. I never fit to their measure of perfection."

"What did I say to make you recall such a thing?"

"The king used to tell me that my reckless heart would kill me. He said I was a creature of the dark."

"You?" Kiah chuckled. "A creature of the dark?"

"You ask me why I hesitate, Kiah. I hesitate because I was insulted for breaking rules. I was insulted for being true to my heart."

"You were raised to serve a cold people in an arrogant court. Forget who you were in the presence of King Averee. Forget who you were in the home of a count." Kiah circled her, reaching to touch her hair with his paint-stained claws. He was covered from head to toe in paint, a wild gleam in his Bat eyes. "You still wish to stay in my cave?" he asked her.

"Yes."

"You wish to learn everything about me?"

"Yes."

Kiah pointed to the canvas. "Bat art is all about a free spirit." He pointed to himself. "I am a free spirit."

At his playful grin, Fly smiled back.

"Do not let the joyful fire fade in you now," he said. "Be wild."

FLY

Paint flew everywhere in the room. Fly found herself caught up in streams of blue, silver, red, and green as she flung brushes and buckets in retaliation for the paint flinging from Kiah's wings. They laughed like children without boundaries, thriving in the present moment of happiness that always seemed fleeting in the great span of life's many sorrows. She did not know a second of Kiah's childhood or if his parents had been as carefree, but there he was, spinning, wings open, eyes overflowing with mischief.

"You are raucous, Kiah," she shouted at him.

"As one should be, little pudding, in the spirit of wit and play."

As Fly flung a brush of yellow paint, Kiah dove forward and grabbed her in his arms, his wings wrapping around her like a stiff, dark cocoon. They were both encircled by the leathery, dragon-sized appendages.

"Is this what you call a Bat hug?" Fly asked from within the shadow of his wings. She smiled up at him.

"You could say that. My wings just did their own thing."

"You didn't make them circle us together?"

Kiah tapped her on the nose with his claw and winked. "I just listened to my senses."

"Can we wash off in the pool?" Fly asked.

"Aye. You don't mind the cold water?"

"I swam in it before, Kiah. I don't mind the cold. You saw me splash about like a fool."

Kiah smiled. "I quite enjoyed watching that."

KIAH

The pool at the bottom of the waterfall was not made for diving, but nonetheless, Fly dove without hesitation into the water. She popped back up to watch Kiah use his wings to glide down and join her. He had shed his tunic and was dressed in only dark leggings as he stood in the pool across from Fly. The waterfall streamed down the tips of his wings and down his hair that laid matted over his eyes.

"Bats are not made to love water, are they?" Fly asked. She wore a thin grey tunic and leggings to maintain purity in his presence.

"Why do you say that?"

"You do not look pleased to stand under cascading water."

"I am savoring it," Kiah said with a serious face. "The dancing in the paint wore me out."

"I didn't think you would be able to last standing up that long."

"My wings are the source of my strength now. They keep me moving."

Fly grinned. "Good thing I pushed you to fly when I did, isn't it?"

"Aye. But all timing comes in its own way."

Perching herself on the grass, legs dangling in the pool, Fly noticed the stillness of the leaves and branches of the plants around them. "Kiah, are there any birds or insects in your garden?"

"Just bats," he said.

"Animal bats? Are there really?" Fly leaned forward, eyes widening.

"Aye. They come when I call them."

"Are they friendly?"

Kiah strode forward in the pool, stretching his wings. "Friendly to those who are friendly to them."

"May I hold one?"

"You do not fear the bats of the wild?"

"I fear no creature, Kiah. Not spiders, or wolves, or snakes. If they wish no harm to me, I will be gentle."

Kiah bowed his head. "Then call them."

"What?"

"Call them with me. Shriek."

"I don't want to disturb the calm—"

"Fly, I haven't heard a single wild sound uttered from you yet." Kiah splashed the water in front of her and bent forward to stare into her eyes. "Shriek. As loud as you can."

<u>FLY</u>

She stood up, turning to face the trees. "Where are they? In what direction?"

"It matters not. Call my bats."

Fly breathed in deep several times and stiffened her shoulders before releasing a guttural, low-toned sound from her mouth.

"No. No, pudding. Higher. Like this." Kiah came next to her, lifting his head and shrieking in a voice that sounded to Fly like a cross between the shattering of ice and a gale force wind.

She did her best to imitate it, and within seconds, dozens of dark-winged bats came flying out of every rock crevice and tree branch.

"Keep still," Kiah said, holding his arm out in front of Fly. "Watch."

He stared up into the flowers of a cherry blossom tree and whispered, "Come, Sieb."

"Is that its name?"

"See-bahs-ake," Kiah said slowly for her. "Siebasacr is the name I gave him two years ago when he came to my cave. The name means 'restless one'."

Fly watched the bat fly down and perch on Kiah's arm. She smiled. "Do they all have names?"

"Not all," Kiah said with a half-smile. "That would take weeks. He is a flying fox, and out of all the bats that come to visit, he seems most attached to me."

"Domesticated?"

"Never, pudding. One never domesticates an animal bat or an Elf Bat. We are born for the wild and we remain as such." He spoke to Siebasacr softly, in what Fly thought to be an unintelligible speech.

"Is that Bat language you speak to him?"

"No. It's an understanding between us. One day you may earn the privilege to learn it." He tilted his head to the side. "You can pet him, Fly."

She reached her hand over the head of the little bat and stroked him, delighted giggles escaping her. "He's beautiful."

Kiah looked up. "Aye. They are." He flicked his wrist upward and Siebasacr took off, disappearing into the trees. "Keep them safe, keep me safe. The life of a Bat is to protect all others from terror."

"It must be a heavy responsibility."

"Sometimes, Fly, I call my bats just to watch them soar around me. Watching them gives me the strength to endure the days preceding my transformation."

"But why must your body weaken like this?"

"It's a part of the change. I am at my most vulnerable," Kiah said as his legs began to shake.

"Why must there be pain to grow? It should not be necessary."

"It is, pudding. One day you will learn what true pain feels like."

Fly propped Kiah up as he began to collapse onto the grass. "I would not wish this transformation on anyone, Kiah," she said.

Working to catch his breath, Kiah let himself fall onto his knees. He arched his back and his wings drooped. "True transformations do not require magic, they require pain." He breathed out hard. "And if I am to be completely transparent, Fly, only now am I learning this lesson. Growth means suffering."

"How do you manage to walk and eat without agony one day, and suffer greatly in the next? Why does your physical pain come and go like this?"

"My body's aches coincide with the state of my mind and heart. I do not know when the next wave of emotion will strike, but when it is a dark feeling, my body weakens."

Fly laid a hand on his shoulder. "I wish I could take your pain."

"You told me that you would not wish my transformation on anyone," Kiah said. "Why would you wish to take my pain onto yourself?"

"I want to see you grow strong. Can't you make your transformation go faster?"

"Magnificent change cannot be rushed, Fly. It can only be endured."

KIAH

When a new daylight came, Fly saw Kiah stumbling around the hearth room, touching imaginary walls, bleary-eyed and moaning from lack of sleep. She set two bowls of lavender pudding down on the table before guiding him to a chair.

"Can't you stop pacing for a moment, Kiah? Your legs keep giving out."

His usual night routine had been to go into his father's

room to rest, but in the past few months, his nightmares had increased alongside his physical pain, making real sleep a terrible joke. On good days he used willpower to make himself do what had to be done, faking a lively spirit so well that Fly hardly noticed when he was on the brink of dreams.

"I heard your cries echo through the cave," Fly said as she lifted her bowl to her mouth. "You have nightmares."

"Neither of us slept last night. Late hours of childish foolishness," Kiah said with a slight smile.

"I am serious. You don't sleep, do you? Not only does your face appear worn from living in pain, but your eyes have lost their sparkle."

"My eyes bore no sparkle to start with."

"Kiah, please tell me. Is it your parents? You miss your mother."

Kiah swallowed and stared at Fly over his bowl. "Nightmares are my reality. Two or three hours of sleep is plenty for a Bat."

"I want to sing for you then," Fly said. She stood and picked up her bowl.

"No. No singing. That cannot stop my dreams."

"What can stop them if not singing?"

Kiah spit purple liquid onto the table. "Do you play anything other than the harp?"

FLY

In his father's room, Kiah laid down on the floor and reached under the bed. He brought back a tin flute and held it up to Fly. "It has been here as long as I can remember, and I am keen to know if it works."

Kiah's momentary boyish demeanor charmed her as she took the flute from him. He wrapped himself in a dark cloak and stared up into her eyes as she remained standing.

"I know one tune," she said. "But it has been years since I played it."

"I'll listen to anything other than a voice," Kiah said. "But I doubt you can put me to sleep, unless it is a flute made by magic."

Fly began to play her song, closing her eyes and swaying atop the rock floor in her bare feet. She fought to keep herself from singing. The king never asked for her voice and neither did her father, but she loved the comfort of uttering words in song.

"I shall not sing a word," she whispered into the dark. "I shall not sing for you." She pressed her lips back to the flute and played softly. She continued to play as the candles flickered down, only faltering when she heard a light snore.

"Sleep well, Kiah," Fly said. She smiled to herself.

KIAH

Waking from his sleep, Kiah crawled out of the room and into the corridor, rising up on unsteady legs. He laid a claw on the wall as he entered the hearth room, surprised to see Fly stirring a pot above a fresh fire. She looked like she belonged there as more than a Bat's caretaker. She looked like a Bat wife. Dirty long hair, a dusty dark cloak draped over her shoulders, the end of it sweeping above her porcelain feet.

"Thank you," Kiah said.

She turned, keeping her hand on the long-handled spoon. "Did you have any nightmares?"

"One. But your presence shortened its hold in my head."

"I stayed with you for an hour," Fly said. She turned back to the fire.

"How long has it been?"

"It's near sunset now."

Kiah crossed his arms over his chest, flexing his claws. He felt blood ooze from his mouth as another new fang sprouted through his gums. The pain sent a shiver through his body.

"You make my cave brighter, Butterfly. Like a living art."

She glanced at him with a smile and laughingly shook her head.

"You are."

"I'm only helping."

"You've done more than any Bat could ask for. And..." he faltered in speech as he watched her glide across the floor to the table. "You're beautiful."

Fly's head snapped up to catch his eyes. He backed away fast, his back hitting the wall. He timidly lowered his head, hair covering the sparkle in his transcendent purple and blue streaked Bat eyes.

"And you, Kiah," she said, "could not be more magnificent. As both a creature of legend and a person to cherish."

Her words soothed and stunned Kiah as he considered moving back toward the table. No living creature outside of his own kind had spoken to him with the gentle valor that she bore.

"What did you make?" he asked, pointing to the table.

"I used what ingredients caught my eye in the garden."

"And?"

Fly stood over the table, head to one side, curls perfectly draped over her purebred Elf ears. "It's lavender mushroom pudding."

"Mixing savory with sweet," Kiah said as he sat down. "I have never tried that before."

"Go on. Tell me if it needs fixing."

He picked up the bowl and brought it to his lips. "Well, my

little pudding, you know how to make a pudding as well as I. And the thought of mixing a mushroom stew with a sweet lavender is more than unique." He made eye contact with her as she watched him. "It's glorious."

"I think you're a better than cook than me," Fly said. She giggled as she slurped her pudding, then swallowed with a grimace. "At least you are good at lying to me."

Kiah shook his head. "I am not fooling you, Fly." At her surprised face, he set down his bowl and reached his arm across the table's surface, laying a claw over her soft hand. "You're beautiful."

9

The Count

Within a fortnight their bond had strengthened, while Kiah's state of body and mind had regressed. Fly became acutely aware of Kiah's physical aches, nourishment needs, and how to thrive as the caretaker of an Elf Bat. She continued to learn to read, skimming pages in more of the ancient Bat books he had shown her. She sneakily cleaned out the bat excrement from every room in the corridor while Kiah bathed in his waterfall pool.

She touched the special objects in his father's room on the hours which she thought he wasn't watching her. The sparkling diadem on the bedside table always caught her attention when she walked by the doorway.

"It belonged to my mother. No one else wears it under my watch, Fly. Leave it be," Kiah would say, his voice harsh only when she dared touch the diadem, eagle-shaped war helmet, or the white cloak laid out on top of the bed. "Go. Out." He would repeat the order until she ducked her head and returned to the hearth room.

Kiah's demands increased during episodes of great physical

agony. His vision had deteriorated to the point where Fly had to place something three inches in front of his eyes, and still it was blurry. His dizzy spells increased when he didn't get a constant drink of blueberry tea. And his gums always bled.

The hours of contentment were few for the Bat, but Fly found him at his most pacified and charming when he worked on one of his paintings. The way in which he held the brushes in his mouth was an art form in itself, and in all the time she spent with him, Fly loved painting the most. There were no rules on Kiah's canvas, and his eyes sparkled as he watched Fly maneuver the brush with her own mouth.

Fly was on her hands and knees observing Kiah in the same position as he painted a forest of squiggly trees full of bats. She moved to sit normally, thinking hard before saying, "I want you to meet my father."

Kiah responded without looking up. "The count?"

"Yes."

"He is not your real father."

"I want him to see that I'm alive."

Kiah spit the brush out and lifted his head. Paint covered the ends of his hair. "I very much doubt that he cares of your life, pudding."

"What does that mean?" Fly asked. She frowned, watching Kiah tuck pieces of hair behind his ear.

"A count of the king is not a deep feeling sort of person. They act based on orders and negative emotion."

"He raised me. I would've died in the wild if he hadn't taken me in as his baby."

"You can go home whenever you want. I will not come."

"Please, Kiah."

"They will attack me." Kiah struggled to stand up, dizziness overtaking him. "They will see me as a monster."

Fly rushed to his side, gripping his arm. "Change their minds. I want him to meet you and for you to prove him wrong."

"I will go under one condition," Kiah said.

KIAH

At the base of the cliff, Kiah and Fly gazed across the stretch of meadow.

"I assume flying is too conspicuous?"

"Aye. I'll call a horse."

"From where?" Fly asked as Kiah backed into the thick of the forest behind them. The collection of trees hugged one side of Ialchagor's Cliff, each one planted centuries ago by ancestors of the Bats.

Kiah returned with a spotted horse following him, bare of a saddle or reins. He saw a look of genuine joy flicker across Fly's face. "This is Gauntlet. He is my steed when the need arises."

Fly hesitated before mounting. "Are you certain you don't wish to wear your normal clothes? An Elf Bat dressed in that way isn't exactly blending in with the purebreds."

"It is different enough for me. I feel safer. Come, pudding, before I turn back for my cave."

He had chosen to disguise himself as a traveling scholar, dressing with what odd pieces he could find in a quick sweep of the corridor's rooms and beneath beds. Thick round-framed glasses, gloves over his claws to create the illusion of long fingers, and light grey clothing with a green cloak made him appear as less of an underworld creature.

"You look like a being from another century, Kiah," Fly said as she joined him on Gauntlet's back. "But I will say that it is a good different. You are a magnificent Elf Bat."

Kiah pushed the hood of his cloak back when they passed through the main gate of Adreachterum, making the choice to dismount with Fly and order his horse to vanish. His vision tunneled as they walked past chattering groups of purebreds, and he felt Fly grab onto his arm to urge him forward.

"It's going to be all right," she told him. She pointed to a gold-roofed house sitting amidst all other uniform structures. "That one."

The feeling he had deep in his stomach as they approached the house reminded him of what he felt as a child on the night of Banegildacht. It was the same fear, the same loss of control. A sense of death. *I can't breathe*, Kiah thought, *I can't do this*. The ground spun beneath him.

"Fly," he started to say, "this is not—"

The door opened to the strong smell of freesia. Kiah found himself standing face to face with Mama's killer.

"Count," Kiah said under his breath. He brought one of his gloved hands to his chest, scrunching the fabric of his cloak. *Count Addis. A murderer.*

The count's eyes drew on him as Fly said, "I'm home, father. This is Kiah."

"Daughter," the count said to her, his eyes not leaving Kiah's face. "I am pleased to know you are well."

Same voice, Kiah thought. Same rings on his hands. Simply dressed, no armor or weapons on him.

"Can we come in?" Fly asked.

The count motioned them forward. "I made enough dinner for several people, although I was not expecting guests." He gave Kiah a half-smile. "Are you the one who mended my daughter?"

"Aye." Kiah glanced around the room to see if there were blades or bows displayed. It was an empty space. Sparse in decoration and color. A purebred home devoid of joy, a spirit of death moving within its walls.

"You knew I was wounded, father?" Fly walked behind the count as he laid out dishes and glasses on a long table.

"I knew the soldiers would attack you. You are a criminal now, my love. You stole property from the king."

Hearing the count's voice made Kiah dizzy. He was a boy again, watching in terror as he learned for the first time how careless one could be with life. Fly spoke to her father as if she believed he was an innocent purebred Elf, as if he still cared for his adoptive daughter's well-being. Fly was ignorant. She was blind to the tragedy of the Bats and deaf to the massacre. But the truth would break her innocence.

"Wine bottles?" Fly said, pointing to one corner. "I thought you didn't like wine, father."

"A recent interest."

"I've only been away for a few weeks and you took up a new drink? I always saw you with fresh berry juice in this house."

"Come now, Butterfly, a lonely male must do what needs to be done to thrive. The letters from your mother don't help me either. Sit, sit, the both of you. Greens and soup are here on the table. I'll get the meat."

As the count left the room, Kiah looked nervously at Fly. He waited for her to sense what he was feeling, to mirror his emotions, but she just smiled. "Kiah, sit. It's all right."

He had no words. Nothing pleasant to say to Fly or her father. His entire body shook as he sat down next to her. Disgust and anger tingled through his limbs and into the wings laid at his back.

The first bites of food were the hardest for Kiah to swallow, but he copied Fly by accepting salad, soup, and a portion of cooked bird that he shoved aside within a second of it touching the plate. Count Addis maintained an agitated expression and dominating body language at the table. Kiah noted each of his movements and kept alert.

"I didn't expect to see you back alive," Addis said as he looked down, aggressively cutting into a piece of dark meat.

"It was not a mortal wound, father."

"No. I only imagined that the king's soldiers knew how to finish the job with one shot."

"Are you saying you wish I wasn't home?"

Addis made direct eye contact with Fly. "I'm saying that I am astounded at the lack of precision." He kept his eyes on her as he brought a piece of meat to his mouth, then flicked his stare to Kiah. "Do you wield a bow, son?"

Kiah tried to hide the tremors in his arms as he held his fork. He clumsily pushed up his thick glasses before answering. "I have blades."

"Good weapons," Addis said. He lifted his wine glass. "Fly, do you have the book with you?"

Fly glanced disconcertedly at Kiah when she heard his fork hit the plate. "No, father. I do not have the king's book."

"Averee will want it. You know that."

"It is not his to keep. It's a cruel text, father."

"Stand against him and his soldiers, child, and risk imprisonment," Addis said coldly.

"He loves my harp-playing. He would never lock me up."

"That book better be brought back in one piece, Butterfly. If it means I go with you to find it, I will do so."

Fly kept her attention fixed on her plate, shoveling forkfuls of meat into her mouth and loudly slurping soup in turn.

"Does the food not sit well with you?" Count Addis waved a

hand over Kiah's plate, seeing that he was only consuming the soup and salad.

"I don't eat meat."

"Not typical in this country, is it, Butterfly?"

Fly put her hand on Kiah's knee under the table. "There are stranger things, father, than a person who does not eat meat."

"Your gums are bleeding, son." Addis smirked as he sipped his wine. "New fangs coming in?"

FLY

The chairs and table rattled from Kiah's violent shaking. Fly couldn't believe what her father had just said.

"Father," she whispered, "you are mistaking my scholar friend for someone else."

"Nothing of the sort." Addis leaned over the table, a frighten-ing gleam in his eyes, wine held high. "Are you sure you don't like meat, Elf Bat?"

"No." Fly watched Kiah stand up and snarl at her father. "No. No, he's not a Bat."

"I knew who you were from the second I saw you in my doorway. Hezekiah, son of Jekkiliah, prince of the Elf Bats." Addis slowly stood as he raised his voice.

Fly gaped up at Kiah. "You're a prince?"

She was ignored as the two of them stared each other down. "He doesn't look like one, does he? I took everything from him and somehow the little Bat survived."

"You slaughtered my family."

"Kiah, he's not a soldier." Fly got to her feet, voice breaking. "He can't be."

"Silence, Fly. You know nothing of pain." Kiah growled like a hungry predator, stern as he swept his attention from Addis to her. "He smells of death."

Terror pushed Fly to back away from the table. She shook her head. "No."

"Don't you know, Kiah," Addis smirked, circling the table, "I kept something from that night?"

He took a small box from a shelf in the corner and opened it on the table. He lifted out Bat fangs and locks of hair. "From your parents. Guess which belongs to whom."

Fly sank against the wall. She listened to her father laugh like a soulless being. Hateful. Empty of love. She felt tears slip down her face as she held back a sob.

KIAH

"You have Kadhle's eyes."

At Addis's words, spoken in pure spite, Kiah released an ear-piercing shriek and charged into Fly, driving his claws into her body. He shook away his glasses, tore off the cloak, and dragged the maiden out of the count's house.

"You're hurting me! Let go, let go of me," Fly pleaded as they rode into the meadow.

Kiah threw her off the horse, rage controlling his entire body. "Your father is a murderer. He must pay."

"No! He is not my father. I didn't know what he did," Fly cried. She scooted backward in the dirt, sobbing as blood trickled from her chest.

"You were in his house. You were raised by the purebred Elf who killed Mama and Father."

"I'm sorry. I'm sorry, Kiah."

"Oh, Fly." Kiah suddenly awoke from his anger and saw the tremor in Fly's hands as she tried to stop the blood soaking through her clothes. "I am not myself," he said. "My little pudding. I am not myself."

"Go." Fly was losing consciousness. She weakly pushed him away as he knelt to touch her.

"You have to go, Kiah. The soldiers can see us from the top of the citadel."

"Let them see," Kiah said. "The time has come."

"What?" Fly moaned as she was lifted into his arms.

"It's time."

"Time for what?"

Kiah waited until her body went limp before he took to the sky, flying straight and high to his cave. "Revenge."

10

Bat's Blood

Fly refused to look in Kiah's eyes when he laid her down in front of the hearth. She drew in trembling breaths as he gently began tending to her wounds and tried not to make a sound in response to the pain.

"I would never harm a Bat," she whispered. "I am not Addis."

"We do not choose our parents, nor do we choose how they act."

Fly heard the cracking in Kiah's voice. As he proceeded to close up the gashes in her body, he spoke in a stern tone. "This is why I have never flown to the city. Everyone in Adreachterum has committed crimes against my people."

"I broke your trust, didn't I?"

Kiah said nothing.

"If I had known what Addis did...."

"I tried to hide my past from you so you wouldn't have to suffer the same nightmares," Kiah said. "If I told you every detail of what I remember, it would bring you great sorrow."

"But I do carry sorrow." Fly winced, feeling Kiah's claws

graze her skin. "I care for you, Kiah. I care for the survival of the Elf Bats. I would not want to see them gone from Sidhovvn."

"Then why did you bring me to the city? "

"I had hoped that I could show him the real Elf Bats," Fly said. "The intelligence, kindness, and protective nature." She looked at Kiah's shadow against the hearth. "He should not have said your mother's name."

"I wish I had not laid eyes on him again. So many years have passed and still the emotions remain the same. He tortured my parents to the point of death."

"I'm not one of those people. I would stand beside you, Kiah, no matter what they said of me. If I had known what he had done, I would have gone to the weapons hoard in his house and drawn his sword—."

"Stop," Kiah pressed his palm flat onto Fly's bandaged wounds. "You would do nothing of the kind."

"I'd do anything to stop him from killing another Elf Bat," Fly said.

"You were the same age as me on that night," Kiah said. "You were an innocent child too."

Fly finally understood. "You acted aggressively in defense of your parents. Your anger has been building up for years." She stared up at him. "Addis unleashed the wild Bat."

"Forgive me," Kiah said softly.

"You have a right to anger."

"There was no war on the Bats. Only a massacre." Kiah sat back on his heels.

Fly saw tears in his eyes. She reached her hand up and held it flat against his chest.

"I'm sorry," she said.

"I won't hurt you again," Kiah whispered. He breathed soft,

staring from her eyes to her mouth until she pulled him down into a kiss.

"I adore you, Fly." He bit her lips gently with his fangs, his own body starting to tremble. He watched her look back at him with soothing eyes. "Is that foolish of me?"

"No," Fly whispered back. "I adore you too."

KIAH

Kiah picked her up in his arms and flew to the top of the cliff. The stars were hidden in the early night sky, covered by thick, swirling clouds.

"It is the Eve of Banegildacht, pudding."

"Bane-gill-dahk?" Fly repeated slowly.

"Aye."

"What is that?"

"It has been twelve years since the slaughter of the Bats. King Averee called it the Death Order. Tomorrow is the anniversary, and each year on this night, I send a candle down the river for my family."

"Is that what sent you into a rage, Kiah? My father insulting your people on this sacred night?"

"Aye. He has disgraced the Bats for the last time." Kiah turned from the cliff's edge to look at Fly. She had stood, wrapping the blanket around herself. "He must pay, pudding. They all must pay."

Fly nodded. She didn't speak.

"Come. I will show you."

Kiah flew her down to the river behind the cave. He pointed to the rushing water. "I send them here." He took an unlit candle from within his tunic and knelt at the river's edge. Another motion of his claws revealed a match and he set the candle alight.

"Let me," Fly said softly. She knelt next to him and wrapped her fingers around his claws. Kiah looked into her eyes as they lowered the candle onto a floating lily pad together.

"Tell me everything," Fly said. "I want to know what happened."

FLY

"*The Royal Methods of Elf Bat Torture*. The dark book of King Averee." Fly heard a growl in Kiah's throat as he said the king's name.

"The one I stole, yes. What about it?"

"It was a text written by his own hand."

"The king wrote it?"

"Aye. He wrote the book after the night of death. It is not an ancient text at all."

"I thought he would have better things to do than write a book."

"Your king is not the most intelligent sort, Fly." Kiah paced back and forth in his garden, the mist of the waterfall dampening his already matted hair. "Nor is he the bravest. I spent years wondering why he didn't become a murderer himself."

"His hands shake. He never could hold a sword."

"Why does he hate my people, Fly? What did my family do to deserve a night of violent death?"

"You did nothing. Maybe he envied your legends. Or perhaps," Fly said, "he thought you were all bloodletters."

Kiah halted his step. "Bloodletters?"

"My father once told me that the king lost his son at the hands of a clan of shadowed creatures called bloodletters. There was a rumor in the city that Elf Bats took part in the killing."

"Impossible," Kiah said. "None of my kin had cruel hearts. All we wanted was longevity and peace in our own communities."

"But now you wish war on the purebreds, do you not?"

"You have no idea what they did. The terrible ways that he ordered the Bloodmanghe to kill."

Fly tilted her head. "Is that the Bat name for soldiers?"

"Aye, they are Bloodmanghe."

"The same soldiers who attacked me on the day I came to your cave?"

"Aye. The same."

Fly nodded at Kiah. "I believe they deserve to pay for their evil."

"But why did they tell you it was a human army that massacred my kin?"

"My adoptive mother was not the kindest person. She left us in a terrible mind. My father said she housed demons."

"So," Kiah said, as he returned to pacing, "would the king have reason to believe that all humans are carriers of evil?"

"She was the only human living among us. I still don't know why Count Addis chose her as his mate."

"Even so, pudding, there are far too many lies in that city. Far too many twisted stories laid out across Sidhovvn. The purebreds must know consequences. Every single one."

Fly arose from her kneeling position and walked toward Kiah. "You speak of the counts."

"Aye. They must know the same suffering of my brethren."

"Banegildacht," Fly said. "It is Bat for Death Order, isn't it?"

Kiah lowered his head. "I wish I could say I am the last to know of Banegildacht, but I am not."

"What does that mean?"

He moved away from Fly to pluck a blossom from a tree.

"Kiah, what is it?"

"There are eight other Bats who were spared that night." He twisted the bloom back and forth in his claws, staring at it intently.

Fly heard only her own breathing and the flow of the waterfall. She saw Kiah was holding his breath. "You mean," she said, coming forward, "you aren't the only survivor?"

"No. I am not." Kiah reached out his claws and wrapped them around Fly's hand. "And there will be ten of us at the end of my hibernation." He looked directly into her eyes.

"You're going to be an Elf Bat, Fly."

KIAH

"What?"

She appeared less afraid than he had anticipated, almost as if the idea instilled hope in her rather than fear.

"It should not be possible, but if it is the truth..."

"We have been bonded since your arrival to my cave, but more than that, it is the kiss we shared that has put your transformation into motion."

At Fly's wide eyes and blushing cheeks, Kiah went on. "It is a phenomenon known in Bat culture as Ilumiaoacht."

"Ill-uhm-aye-oh-ahk," Fly echoed.

"Aye. It means 'unified purity'. I want you to be my wife, and before I even hear your response, I can feel in your body that you want the same. Tell me. Am I right?"

"You are right. I want to be your she-bat, Kiah."

"You will be." He drew her in close, leaning down to press his forehead against hers. "You are going to be my little pudding forever."

Meek, childlike Fly smiled up at him. He could feel her joy, wrapped in his embrace. But within an hour of returning to the hearth room, Kiah's limbs began to convulse, chills wracked his core, and he collapsed.

11

The Marriage

"Coalhsomeii," a familiar voice called out. "Tis close to the time, is it not?"

Kiah opened his eyes. A blurred figure strode toward him and Fly, and the sound of jingling earrings followed.

"Spindle," Kiah breathed out. He felt Fly grasp his arm tightly. "My old friend."

"Astounding." Spindle cocked his head. "There is a female purebred in your house," he said, halting in disbelief between each word. "Or is this a new trick brought by the magic water?"

"She needed rescuing."

"You left your cave? It's been near a full month and you accomplished more than I imagined you would in six months."

"Call her my good luck charm, Spindle. This is Fly."

Fly stood and shyly smiled at the pirate. She started to offer her hand when he stepped forward with open arms.

"Hello, Spindle," she said quietly amidst the zealous embrace.

Spindle drew back, touching Fly's hair and face. "A real female in Kiah's cave."

"Aye, Spindle," Kiah said from his position on the floor. "Ease up on her."

"Did you think I wasn't coming back? I had promised that I would."

"Your timing, cabin boy, is impeccable."

Spindle grinned broadly at the two of them as Fly returned to Kiah's side. "How long have you two known each other?" he asked.

"Since the day you left me," Kiah said.

"That's nothing short of a miracle, Bat. But you know as well as I, time is ending for wasteful pleasure. Your limbs are at their weakest and you cannot stand without the room spinning." He turned to Fly. "He must depart from us, love. And we from him."

Fly nodded. "I understand."

"Do you?"

"Yes."

"If you are the one who got him to step outside this tragic cave, I owe you more than a drink."

"You may as well know, Spindle," Kiah said, "that she pushed me to fly."

Spindle's eyes widened as he looked at Kiah. "You flew?"

"Aye. Thanks to Fly's reckless impulses."

Spindle gave Fly another toothy grin. "Power to you, love," he said with a wink. Fly blushed, biting back a smile as she ducked her head.

"Help me up." Kiah leaned on both Fly and Spindle as they pulled him to his feet. He glanced down to see them both looking up at his pained expression, concern showing on their own faces.

"I have one thing to complete here, Spindle, before you bring her to meet the other surviving Bats. I wish you to marry us."

"You're joking, Bat."

"No." Kiah smiled down at Fly. "She's my love."

"Please," Fly chimed in, her voice tender.

Spindle backed away, pointing a finger at each of them in turn. A sly smile came over his face. "So...you two have...."

"No. We have not!" Kiah barked at him. "We shared one kiss. And before we go further, I want her to be my wife. You know the Bat standards."

"Of course I do. I heard all about it. But you are in love? Bonded forever? For certain?"

"No doubt, Spindle," Kiah said to him, then gazed into Fly's eyes. "She's the last she-bat."

Spindle appeared both touched and amused as he said, "Fly, welcome to the family."

Kiah cut him off from going in for another hug. "Wait for her to meet the others, Spindle. You are as rowdy as ever. Now, do we get a wedding or not?"

"Aye, Bat. It shall be done." He crooked a finger at Fly. "You, Miss Fly, must come with me."

FLY

"This was one of his mother's cloaks. Lucky thing the soldiers did not take everything on that night."

"Bloodmanghe," Fly said as she looked at her reflection in the mirror.

"Bloodmanghe, yes." Spindle seemed surprised. "How do you know the proper name for the soldiers?"

"Kiah has been teaching me ancient Bat text."

"You sound so much like Kadhle, love. The strength of your voice is just as hers was. She could gather two hundred Bats for a feast with a single syllable, and it was never an ear-piercing screech. It was always rolling, musical, like a lullaby."

Fly slowed her breathing as Spindle deftly wove pins into her hair. "Like when she sang Ialchagor?"

"How do you know that?" Spindle asked.

"I'm not supposed to know it. Kiah says he does not remember her singing it, but I want to carry the song."

"There is no way he could forget his mother's voice. K'adhlenalde was beyond an ethereal angel. I remember every song that came from her mouth."

Fly whirled to face Spindle as he was about to place a familiar diadem on her head. "Kiah does not want anyone else to wear that. Only his mother."

"On your wedding day, it is fitting." Spindle waited for her to turn back to the mirror. "Besides, love, he will be too filled with joy to be angry about it."

"How is he going to make it through the ceremony in his condition?"

"I mixed a special medicine in his tea. He will last through the night."

"All night?"

"Trust me, you will both need it." He winked at her reflection. "Tonight is for love and consummation. Tomorrow," he said, his voice suddenly somber, "tomorrow is going to be a rough ride."

Fly touched the cloak at her shoulders, twisting her body to the side to watch it brush across the floor. She smiled at the female she saw in the mirror. Spindle stood a few inches shorter than her, securing the decorations to her hair.

"Are you ready for this?" he asked.

"You doubt my capabilities, Spindle."

"I doubt your pain tolerance. Life as a she-bat is the opposite of glorious. And being the wife of a crabby Bat prince isn't a dose of sunshine either."

"I can do this. He is my world."

"A single commitment for a lifetime is a rare thing. But if you are to be his mate, Fly, he is a lucky soul."

KIAH

At the edge of the river where they had released a candle for the dead, Kiah lovingly gazed into the eyes of his precious Fly. They both wore white cloaks over pale blue bodysuits. The tree branches hung thick over their heads, but the stars still shone through and sparkled on the water.

"We are gathered here to celebrate and unify two magnificent loves." Spindle glanced behind him. "Pretend we have a crowd."

Fly giggled and Kiah rolled his eyes. "Go on, Spindle."

"Hezekiah, repeat these words: I will stand for purity, morality, and justice in love."

"I will stand for purity, morality, and justice in love."

"I will follow you into battle."

"I will follow you into battle."

"Never forsaking my love for you."

"Never forsaking my love for you."

Spindle turned to Fly. "Butterfly, repeat these words: I will follow you into battle."

"I will follow you into battle."

"I will protect you, respect you, and honor you with my love."

"I will protect you, respect you, and honor you with my love."

"My family is your family."

"My family is your family."

He turned back to Kiah. "Hezekiah, repeat after me: I will guide you through every valley and carry you up every mountain."

"I will guide you through every valley and carry you up every mountain."

"I will keep you safe."

"I will keep you safe."

"I will fly beside you forever."

"I will fly beside you forever."

Spindle gave them each a serious look. "Repeat this together: You are my home."

Kiah smiled wide, fangs gleaming. Fly held tight to his claws, smiling back. "You are my home."

"Ilumiaoacht."

"Ilumiaoacht," they whispered in unison.

"Kiss your wife, Bat, and I'll leave you two be for the night."

"Aye, Spindle," Kiah said. "You'd best lock yourself inside the cave, for there will be a storm of love out here."

Spindle started to walk away but suddenly swung around on his heel. "Oh, wait. I almost forgot something." He dug into his pocket and took out two sapphire rings, holding them in his palms. "Courage ring for the groom, courage ring for the bride. Consider this my wedding present."

Kiah came forward, grabbing one of the rings to study it. "These are Mama and Father's rings." He met Spindle's eyes. "Where did you find them?"

"You know me, Bat." Spindle shrugged with a grin. "I always left your cave with a trinket in my pocket. I found them near the hearth on the night of Banegildacht, and since then, I have carried them with me for safekeeping."

"Thank you."

"You are worthy of wearing them, the both of you. Now, go on with her." He backed away, his mischievous grin disappearing in the night. "Make the love."

The second kiss of the Bat prince and his wife endured in the darkness of the forest, the purity of their passion and adoration echoing through Ialchagor's Cliff.

12

Hibernation and Sanctuary

FLY

"This is where we leave you." Spindle dismounted and followed Kiah to a clearing in the thick trees. "I promise to keep her safe."

Kiah gripped his hand with his claw and grinned. "Just keep the boys in line while I'm gone. And if you are to take off yourself, Spindle, I trust you will pass the torch to Snowblind. He is the wisest of the eight."

"Of course. Safe journey, Kiah." Spindle backed up toward his horse, watching Fly go to her husband.

"Return to me." Fly looked up into his eyes as he embraced her. "Do what you must do and come home."

"I will, my little pudding." Kiah tapped her nose with the tip of his claw. "Listen to my brethren." He cupped her chin and kissed her. "Fly for me, Fly."

Fly watched him disappear into the forest, dark cloak swirling behind him.

"Let's ride on," Spindle said. "Come, love."

The path to the Underground Sanctuary was a calm, flat

terrain through forest the entire way. Sunlight filtered through the treetops, the leafy branches so dense that little of the blue sky could be seen.

"What happens to Kiah when he is transforming?"

"Coalhsomeii is like a butterfly mixed with a bear. Hibernation, chrysalis, a rebirth."

"Will he remember me?"

"Don't fear, love. Kiah will not forget either of us. He will have the same mind and same heart. It is only his body that is changing. He will return to us stronger."

"Are we going to discuss revenge against the king?"

"So many questions," Spindle said with a sigh.

"Will the other Bats be as kind?"

"They will cherish you the same, Fly. You are becoming one of them as we speak. Within the hour you will feel a pain vibrating through your bones and you shall not be shocked since I told you."

Fly didn't wait long to ask her next question. She was fascinated by Spindle, and part of her did not want to acknowledge the agony that was coming. "How long have you been a pirate?"

"I was born on the sea to a pirate captain's wife. He was human, she was Elf. She brought me to land and raised me in a treehouse near Kiah's cliff."

"You mean Ialchagor's Cliff?"

"Yes," Spindle said. "I met Kiah when he was only two years old. I was five. His parents kept a strong friendship with my mother."

"What was Kadhle like?"

Spindle slowed his horse, turning around to look at Fly. "He didn't tell you about his mother?"

"I know her name but few things about her. He won't discuss

his parents with me."

"K'adhlenalde was stunning. The queen of the Bats. Kiah was very attached to her as a child, and it is likely he saw and realized what had happened to her right before she died."

"What happened?"

Instead of answering, Spindle brought his horse into a brisk trot, increasing the distance between himself and Fly.

"Spindle," Fly called, urging her horse after him. "What happened to Kiah's mother?"

Spindle halted his horse and dipped his head. "The counts violated the females. Even the very young."

"Why?"

"I don't know. Every action they took that night was unwarranted." He rode forward, shoulders stiffening.

"Is that why there are only male Bats left? Because the females died under the mark of dishonor?"

"They were not only violated, Fly. They suffered the worst torment by every weapon. As their children watched, the mothers had their wings torn from their bodies, fangs torn from their mouths, and the young females were burned alive. Every Bat died under circumstances I cannot even rightly explain to you."

Fly kept to herself for a while, thinking through everything Spindle had told her. Finally, a flicker of recognition showed on her face. "The king didn't want any females left alive to bear future Bat heirs. That's why they were all wiped out."

"That is true, love. Each of the Bats you will meet at the Sanctuary come from separate bloodlines and they all have seen terrible violence committed against their families. Some bear physical scars from that night, others suffer recurring nightmares such as Kiah does. Allow them their space and time as they get to know you. It is not natural for any purebred Elf to become a Bat."

"But it has been done before, hasn't it? A purebred female becoming an Elf Bat?"

"Only one other time that I know of," Spindle said.

"And how did she turn out?"

"She was slaughtered on Banegildacht."

At his sharp gaze, Fly lowered her eyes and slowed to move her horse back behind his.

"We're close now, love. The gate is a few more paces northwest."

The entrance gate of the Sanctuary sloped down into a tunnel, and the tunnel appeared to narrow before spreading out like a funnel in the dirt.

"I promise it's larger inside than it looks out here," Spindle said as he dismounted.

Fly started to slide to the ground but stopped when she felt a pulsing pressure inside of her mouth. She raised a hand to her face.

"Spindle?"

"What is it? We need to get you settled before the other Bats join us."

"Spindle," Fly said again, "my teeth feel loose."

The half-breed pirate looked over his shoulder at her. "Spit," he said.

Fly spat into her hand and was horrified to see two teeth fall out onto her palm. "No." She shook her head. "That's not possible."

"A whole new set of chompers is coming in, love. Not to mention, all of them will be retractable fangs."

"I'm not losing all my teeth this way." Fly continued to look down at her hand and back at Spindle who stood at the gate chuckling. "Why are you laughing?"

"If you don't complain half as much as Kiah did, I will be amazed. I warned you the transformation was starting."

Fly frowned and covered her mouth as she leapt to the ground. She adjusted the pack across her shoulder and followed Spindle toward the tunnel.

"Is there a password?"

"No word. Only a gatekeeper. Saedha."

"Say-ee-thah," Fly repeated slowly.

"Aye. A gobliness and ally of the Bats. She is very old. Over five hundred years."

Spindle was the first to greet Saedha the gatekeeper when she unlocked the inner door. The space inside was indeed larger to stand at full height, though as Fly glanced around the front room, she wondered if all eight of the full-grown Bats could fit without being forced to hunch.

"Saedha, this is Butterfly."

Fly bowed, then blushed when Saedha bowed in return.

"I am no royal, Miss Gobliness."

"You are," she said in a gentle, husky voice. "Wife of Hezekiah. Welcome to the Underground Sanctuary." She bowed again.

Fly looked sideways at Spindle who subtly shook his head at her to refrain from another bow.

"What do you call this room?"

"Meeting room," Saedha said. "Table big enough for a dozen bodies to sit and a hearth warm enough to heat the whole of the Sanctuary."

"All one floor," Spindle said to Fly as they followed the gobliness past the long table and hearth.

"How does one have a fire in an underground home?"

"And yet you had no qualm about a fire inside a cave?"

"I have no worry about it. I am only curious, Spindle."

"Let's just call it magic," Spindle answered with a roll of his eyes. "Come."

Saedha's skin was rough and scaly, an olive-green tint. Her hair was curled, styled in a low bun with bangs swept to one side above her gold eyes. The goblin race rarely lived among surface communities, but Fly learned that Saedha had been providing a safe haven for Bats for centuries.

"This is where a troubled Bat could come and seek guidance, solitude, and rest for months at a time. And now, at last, you are here to meet the last survivors of the massacre," Spindle said to Fly.

"When do they come?"

"I'd say," Spindle began, turning his head to the open door, "that they are here."

SNOWBLIND

On the hour which the world falls away in the spirit of war, an unkempt beauty will shine down the valley and through each corridor at the citadel's base. Snowblind closed the notebook he held in his claw as he entered the meeting room. The first thing he saw was the wife of Hezekiah standing timidly next to the half-breed pirate. *This is the new Bat queen*, he thought. *Butterfly.* She was not at all what he had predicted her to be.

"Spindle, it has been a good many years."

"Aye. You, Snow, look quite aged yourself."

Snowblind removed his rectangle-framed glasses and huffed at the pirate. "I'm certain I do. This is our Fly, is it not?"

Fly lowered her eyes when he stepped up to her. "I am."

"I am Snowblind."

"Master," she whispered, bowing deep.

He looked over at Spindle who silently shrugged, then looked back at Fly. "Seeing as you are in the beginning of your transformation, I would get comfortable looking ugly in our presence."

Fly snapped her head up and Snowblind grinned at the shock on her face. "Aye, girl, I can read your thoughts. You hate having no control of your delicate, purebred body falling apart on you, but unsightly changes will be happening every day that you are here."

"How do you do that?"

"All Bats can sense each other's thoughts. It's the animal bond. I thought Kiah would have taught you as much."

Fly shook her head and her face flushed with color. "No magic?" she asked him, staring up at his hollow cheeks and rough-skinned neck.

"No magic," Snowblind said. "We sense emotion before anything else." He started to take a seat in one of the chairs at the table, pausing to watch Fly close her eyes and take a loud, deep breath in the middle of the room. "Girl, I would not try mind-reading yourself. It would only give you a massive headache. Wait until you mature."

The blue color of her eyes reminded him so much of his wife and daughters. He put his glasses back onto his nose. *Adreinnha,* Snowblind wrote in his notebook, *tell the girls how much I love them.* He stepped back outside to rip the page out, pressed his lips to it, and let the wind take it from his claw.

<u>FLY</u>

Fly stood by the door, anxious for the company of her future brethren. She did not yet feel the kinship that she wanted to as a Bat, but she hoped that she would soon come to understand their pain. Snow did not feel warm in the slightest. His eye colors were pale, shadowed hues, his bone-white hair long at his back. His body language echoed the prior sorrow of Kiah, as unfeeling as any living thing could be in the introduction of new life.

He must have his reasons, Fly thought. She wanted to believe what Spindle had told her of the terrible torture, but in the throes of her own physical hurt, she could only think of her own discomfort. Each Elf Bat that entered the Underground Sanctuary had a somber air about him, a beautiful, tragic shadow on his face. As Spindle had said, some bore physical scars from that night, and others appeared untouched by blade or flame, only revealing their pain when they opened their mouths to speak.

The next Bat who entered had large azure blue and flame orange streaked eyes, hypnotizing to look at despite a cloudy film across them. His ears twitched in the direction of each voice in the room. Without being told, Fly realized that he was completely blind.

"This is Tsunami," Spindle said from behind her. "He's twenty-one years old."

"Master," Fly said, standing still as he took a step forward and reached out his right arm.

"Call me Soo," he said in a profoundly lilted, musical voice. He felt the smoothness of her cheek and the tangle of her curls with his claw. "You have a long way to go, dearest, to the end of your transformation."

Fly didn't speak as he moved past her, but she glanced at him over her shoulder. Soo's fine blond hair laid neatly down his back with no decoration or braids. His attire showed a refined simplicity, his voice akin to a gentle wind blowing against glass chimes.

"Nice to be in the warmth," Soo said to Spindle.

"Looks like Tor and Ty were right behind you," Spindle said.

Fly backed up against the wall as two more Bats crossed the threshold. They both had dark complexions and matching silver circlets upon their heads.

"You must be Fly," one of them said to her. He traded grins with the other. "Isn't she pretty?"

"She is," the other said. "Kiah chose his female well."

"Typhoon and Tornado," Spindle said to Fly. "Twenty-two and twenty-one."

"Are you brothers?" Fly asked them.

"We are not. Separate bloodlines, my love."

"Your faces, clothing, even your mannerisms, it all looks the same."

"Perhaps," Tornado said with a playful wink, "it appears the same to confound an enemy."

"Gracious girl," Typhoon said, "I know how it looks from the exterior, but get to know us one at a time and you will get to know two very different Bat warriors."

They both had deep, bold voices overflowing with a dry, firecracker-edged wit. Tornado had cornflower blue and citrine yellow streaked eyes, and his hair was a dull ebony hue, chopped above the shoulders. Typhoon had tangerine orange and rose pink streaked eyes, his hair a cedar brown and styled in a low bun with strands framing his firm jawline.

"You can call us Tor and Ty."

Fly gave them a small smile and a shallow bow. "Masters."

They went past her to the long table, loudly greeting Snowblind and Soo.

"The love of Hezekiah," the next Bat outside the door said to Fly.

"Master," Fly whispered to him, starting to hold out her arm. "Do you need help to get inside?"

"I can make it alone, beauty." He rested the left side of his body on the doorframe and smiled, revealing a missing canine fang. "I'm Hurricane. Caine."

Fly kept close to him as he came inside, watching him shift his weight back to his right side. Caine was missing his right arm and leg, relying on half a wooden staff as a replacement for his bottom limb.

"Twenty-two years old," Spindle said of him. "And aren't you looking well-rested."

"Always joking, aren't you, pirate? It was a long journey without taking flight. But the physical exertion was needed. I've been sleeping too much."

Fly watched him gracefully move on one leg, silently wondering of his past and what he had endured. Caine had plum purple and mint green streaked eyes, cloud-white hair flowing freely past his shoulders, and on the top of his left hand, just above the place where the knuckles melded into his claw, was a faded tattoo, the shape of it unfamiliar to Fly.

"And so it begins," called out the next Bat who strode through the door. "The newest member of the family is with us." He flamboyantly bowed to Fly. "I'm Firestorm, but the others call me Fire."

"How old are you?"

"Nineteen."

Fly found Fire's appearance to be a strange mixture of boyish and ferocious. He had waist-length, fawn brown hair with tiny braids throughout, and his stern, high-arching eyebrows contrasted to the baby fat in his cheeks. The expressions made with his brows and eyes were more intense than that of his rounded jawline and terribly misaligned fangs, the canines overgrown and incisors having large gaps between them. He had the sort of eyes that you did not want to see standing over you whilst aiming a blade or bow, irises colored in pristine streaks of tiger orange and grasshopper green. He appeared to be the most keen-sighted of all the Bats, and considering how the vision of Bats weakened in their adult years, his was remarkable.

"Fire, you dancing scoundrel," Snow said as he embraced him by the table. "Upset any more celebrations in Sidhovvn with your fog-crafting wings?"

Fly saw smiles light up their faces as they joked together, transforming the atmosphere in the room from melancholy to merry. As more of them arrived, the Bats seemed comforted and content. It was as if the playful animals in them were brought to life out of a deathly, tearful rest.

"Avalanche," Spindle called out over the loud antics of Ty and Tor. He bobbed his head to the side when he had Fly's attention again, gesturing toward the next Bat's arrival.

"Master," Fly said. This time she met the new Bat before he stepped inside. She felt the fabric of his cloak brush against her as he mirrored her bow with his own.

"Mistress Fly," Avalanche said gently. "You may call me Vale."

"Vale, I am honored to meet you."

"As am I in your presence, dear Butterfly. Kiah chose well. You're lovely."

Fly blushed hard as she let him move past her, awed by the staunch, stolid features of his face. Vale had prominent cheekbones and a rigid jawline, and his eyes were charcoal grey and sunflower yellow streaks. He carried a different type of weight in his shoulders as he walked, a sorrow that seemed to weigh down bone and muscle, making him appear far older than he was. His hair was a filthy straw-blond color and tied in a single, thick braid at his back.

"Vale is twenty-four years," Spindle said to Fly. "Another magnificent survivor."

"Thank you, Spindle," Vale said. "Though your compliments are not necessary."

"Only helping to clarify for the lady." Spindle grinned playfully at Fly before retreating into the kitchen with Saedha.

The energy in the room shifted like a sea tide in wind when the fringe of the final Bat's cloak crossed the threshold. He stood resolute, his polar white and crimson red streaked eyes scanning the entire group inside. His hair was the color of dried blood, only growing long on the right side of his head, a tiny braid laying in the middle of the smooth locks. He had long earrings like Spindle, but instead of being hooked at the earlobe, they dangled from the tips of his pointed ears. The jingly, chain ornaments were a charming way to distract from the burn scars that covered his face and looked to be traveling down his tunic to every other part of his body.

"Volcano," Tsunami said. "The baby. Sixteen years old, and a rare example of a full-fledged Bat before the age of eighteen."

Volcano was the most outwardly disfigured of them all, yet his face exuded unrelenting joy when he set his eyes on Fly.

"Hello, Butterfly." He bowed deep. "I hear you are our new queen."

VULKIE

92

The shock on Fly's face amused him as he waited for her to speak. She scanned the room for Spindle, her eyes landing on the pirate casually reclined in a lone chair by the hearth. He spooned a watery stew into his mouth, giving her a nod when she caught his eye.

"What's that look for?" Spindle asked Fly, broth dripping off his spoon as he held it in mid-air.

"I just…I…" Fly looked at each of the Bats who now wore the same amused expression as Volcano. "I'm your queen?"

The sweet, feather-soft tone of her voice reminded Volcano of Mama's singing. The last time he had heard a lullaby was on Banegildacht, the words of Ialchagor sung hoarsely through the burning trees to his scorched four-year-old ears. Part of him now wanted to hear Fly sing a song, to see if she sounded just like Mama.

"When Kiah returns, aye, it is official. He is no longer a prince."

"Your deep bond with him," Vale said, "solidified your becoming Bat queen. From the first kiss."

Fly frowned at Spindle who calmly ate his stew. "You all knew this."

"Dearest," Soo said, "why is being queen any more startling than becoming a Bat?"

"It's just…" Fly looked down at the floor, crossing one arm over her chest. "The duties, the responsibilities. There is so much to know if I am to become…queen." She lifted her head and met Volcano's eyes as a grin spread across his face, a set of crowded fangs glistening in the dim light.

"We make a glorious entrance, don't we, lovie? Call me Vulkie." He grabbed her in a hard embrace, feeling her hesitation. "I'm the fun one," he whispered into her ear.

"Good to know," Fly said, returning his embrace. She gave a shy smile as he stepped back to acknowledge the others.

"Come," Spindle said. "Saedha brings food. We have much to discuss."

"Tell me this won't be a six hour meeting," Vulkie groaned as he sat himself next to Fire at the long table. "Spindle, why bother joining us if you are eating on your own?"

"Stew is not a dinner. It's a prelude. And I don't consider fruit, puddings, or salads a well-balanced meal for my uses."

"If you wish to poke fun at our diet," Fire stated, "go eat an ounce of meat in your own corner."

Spindle defensively lifted his hands, one hand smoothly grabbing a tankard of ale from Saedha as she passed by. "I am not poking fun. I know I can eat meat anytime I want. But tonight is for our Fly to progress in her physical transformation and learning of Bat history."

"To speak of Banegildacht," Caine added.

"Exactly."

By the time Saedha had laid out each serving dish, half the food had already been hoarded onto the plates. Vulkie, out of habit, held up a fistful of berries, ready to instigate a food fight. But in the presence of the wide-eyed, blushing queen, and at a stern look from Saedha, he sheepishly decided against causing a larger commotion.

He found himself drawn to Fly, watching her curious expressions from across the table. He hoped she could not yet sense his thoughts the way he could sense hers. She was curious of his scars, of that he knew, and from what he could follow in her mind, she was wondering about his parents, siblings, and how he had survived at all.

<u>FLY</u>

Having been brought together, the Bats were a boisterous, mannerless lot, behaving like mischievous boys at the table. The chaos of eight male Bats in one room would have been startling for any rule-abiding purebred, but for Fly, watching and listening to their unified antics proved the greatest entertainment of her life.

"I could tell you what you are thinking, Miss Fly," Fire said from across the table. He traded a wink with Vulkie. "But it will serve you better to speak it yourself."

By the look of the table, Fly noted that none of the Bats drank or smoked in the manner that Spindle was currently indulging. She concluded to herself that any Bat who only drank tea and kept to a vow of purity would also answer a question truthfully.

"How do you know each other if not by family ties?"

"Animal instinct," Fire said. "When you are one with your breed, you can always sense their mental state, their fear and agony. It was amplified on Banegildacht in such a way that none of us could escape the pain. Those who survived, all nine of us, were writhing and weeping for each other. We had never met before that night." His eyes shifted from Fly to the Bat sitting at her left. Snowblind.

"A survivor always recognizes another survivor," Snow said. "We can feel them."

Fire nodded and, after seeking Fly's face for contentment, he returned to forking bits of salad with his claws.

"Does that mean you all chose to pledge purity at the same time?"

"We are pledged to a life of celibacy and purity to honor our females who were violated on Banegildacht." Vale spoke into his cup. "It is a vow we do not take lightly."

Spindle lifted his tankard at the head of the table as Saedha refilled his ale. "On the note of saving oneself in purity, I have something to say about Kiah and Fly's bond. One month is short. Remarkably short."

The looks on the faces of the Bats suddenly turned aggressive. "What do you know about courting a female, pirate? Any love will take years to strengthen, of course. But in our culture it is something far different from what you know as true love."

"Elaborate," Spindle said, not entirely paying attention to Vale.

"A month of courting is a generous time before marriage," Tor said. "When you know, you just know."

"My mother and father married within two weeks of knowing each other," Caine said from the other end of the table.

Spindle snorted into his ale. "That is hardly sane."

"They lasted, my friend. Each heart connection is different."

"Have you found love?" Soo pointedly asked Spindle.

"Not as deeply or as rapidly as anyone here."

"That's enough love talk," Snow said, forming his right claw into a fist on the center of his plate. "Get to the urgent matter."

"Right then." Spindle stood up, leaning to one side with his empty tankard in hand. "Saedha, more ale!"

"No need to shout, pirate."

"Aye. All right." He shook his hair out over his eyes, earrings jingling, and once Saedha refilled his ale, he spoke again. "To the gathering of the last Bat warriors. May revenge be—"

"Pardon," Vale interrupted. "Warriors out of necessity would be the proper statement." He stirred sugar into his tea as he looked around the table. Fly noticed the delicate cup clattering about, apple tea dripping everywhere. By the time Vale would stop stirring to take a sip, there would be nothing save for a few drops left in the cup. "None of us were built for a life of war," he said.

Fly had not eaten a bite of food since they had all sat down. Loosening teeth and a nervous stomach kept her from ingesting anything except tea. She looked at the bowl of untouched pudding that was set before Vulkie. He met her eyes and seemed to know her thoughts, grinning as he pushed it toward her.

"Has no one at this table killed another?" she asked with a thankful tilt of the head to Vulkie. She lifted the pudding to her mouth hesitantly, hoping her teeth would stay in place as she ate it.

"I have," Snow said. "And even in the absence of intentional violence, I know my brethren will act swiftly to defend their dead's honor."

"If I may finish," Spindle said, his words beginning to slur, "The eight of you have come for one purpose. To defend your king and queen."

"To honor our dead," Caine said.

"You have been living in silent isolation since Banegildacht. You are survivors of the greatest massacre in Sidhovvn, and now is the time for resurgence."

Fly saw Fire roll his eyes. "We know this, Spindle. We know why we are here."

"But," Fly interrupted, "this was a massacre of the king's order. Why were you spared? You should all be dead. Kiah should be dead."

"Meaning what?" Snow asked, eyes stern as he looked at her.

Fly felt an air of frustration forming between them. Snow's arm that had brushed against hers a moment ago was now pressed to his chest in a state of icy distrust. He was close to falling off his chair, his body awkwardly twisted away from her.

"I speak of the Bloodmanghe," she said. "They had orders to kill. The counts had orders to kill. Why would they leave anyone alive on purpose?"

"One last fight," Vale said. "That's what they want."

"Aye," Tor said. "The king wants us to attack to prove him right about us being bloodletters."

"It's a trap then."

"No." Spindle's body swayed as he set his ale down. "Kiah meant for a resurgence. His transformation has always meant that this day would come. Fly's arrival set the final stage for our attack. Revenge is long overdue."

Ty grinned and all the Bats looked at Fly. "I'd say she was right on time."

"But I knew nothing of Banegildacht prior to meeting Kiah. I knew nothing of the truth of the Elf Bats, or that I would become one."

Caine stood up, gripping the back of his chair. "Knowledge or lack of knowledge does not determine the outcome, Fly. It just is."

"Who do you blame for the massacre?" Fly asked.

"No one is to blame except the soul who spoke the order."

"Averee," Fly whispered.

"Aye. He is bitter toward any creature who doesn't acknowledge his rule."

Tor spoke before he slurped more of his stew. "Spindle tells us your father was the one who ordered the slaughter of Kiah's parents."

"He did," Fly replied without hesitation. "But he is not my blood."

"And your mother, we hear, is human. They adopted you?"

Fly sensed a guarded energy in the room. "I was given to them after they lost their blood son in a wildfire. My mother begged for King Averee to find them a boy, but all they got was me."

"Why was it Averee's duty to find them a child?" Vale asked.

"She was barren. Then she left my father and I when I was five years old. My father said it was because she was full of demons. They never spent one night without screaming at each other."

"Aye," Snow said into his tea. "I'm sure it was demons. In my lifetime I've found human females to be the most irrational of beings regardless of a dark influence."

The Bats were all looking at Fly as she watched Snow rise from his chair and back away from the table, teacup in claw. His eyes were troubled.

"Snow hates humans," Fire said. "A pack of them killed his grandparents the day before Banegildacht took the rest of the family."

"Why?"

"They drained blood from my grandfather hoping to attain his immortality for themselves." Snow growled, looking at Fly. "Foolish humans never learn. Both the assassins who attacked were female. If your human mother left you in such a rage, girl, I do not doubt that she will return the same way."

"I do not understand, Master Snow," Fly said. "Why would she come back? She was angry. My father said she did not love."

"The job is never finished until the pain is gone. If she blames the king for failing to protect her blood son and for not giving her the child she wanted after his death, revenge is overdue for Ixetmori. She will come." Snow came back to the table, standing right over Fly as she gaped up at him. "And all of Sidhovvn will pay, my dear."

I hope you are wrong, Fly thought. She saw him subtly shake his head for her alone to notice. The threat of Ixetmori returning was the least of their problems, but from what Snow told her through the gleam in his eyes, the wrath of the humans was near.

VULKIE

"So," Ty spoke up, "where do we go from here?"

"We do nothing until Kiah returns," Caine said, impatiently flexing his lone left arm on the table.

"What if he doesn't come back on time?"

"He will." Vale half-smiled. "Don't worry about that, Fire."

"This attack must happen on a midnight."

"It will."

"You all have a task while we wait for Kiah," Spindle said. He had silently followed the conversation of the Bats, drunken eyes shifting from one to the other at the table. "You train his bride."

They all looked at Fly, color rising in her cheeks again.

"You decide amongst yourselves who will train her in what," Spindle said. "But time is short, and she must master it all."

"Spindle," said Tor, his overbite prominent as he stood up to glower at him. "How is it that we do all the work and you do nothing?"

"I also have work, Bat," Spindle said, head tilted back to look in his eyes. "I will gather my crew for Kiah's return. We have our own training to complete."

"Fair enough," Tor conceded. He walked away from the table toward the hearth.

Vulkie watched Spindle motion with a finger for Fly to follow him to the door.

"Vulk, you feeling up to a round of sword practice before sleep?" Fire asked.

"Shh." Vulkie held up a hand. "Wait."

"What?"

"Just shh, Fire." He got up as the other Bats quietly mingled near the hearth, eyes on Spindle and Fly. He stilled his head and jingly earrings in order to hear the words spoken between them.

"Love, there is one last piece of advice I have to give you," Spindle said.

"What is it?"

Spindle went on with a stoic face. "Don't turn your back on Snow."

Fly gave him a quizzical look as the pirate leaned in close and whispered into her ear, "he will be the hardest to crack."

Vulkie cocked his head, seeing both of them look at Snowblind where he sat, arms crossed. He was frowning at Fly.

Spindle drew Fly in for an embrace with one arm, then pushed her back. "I'll see you, Fly."

Suddenly he was out the door, and Fly's back was turned to every Bat in the room. As she watched the pirate leave, Vulkie could see the tension in her shoulders, the tremble in her hands.

FLY

Fly felt sixteen eyes on her as she slowly turned around. A wind blew through the open doorway as she stood feeling vulnerable and tiny against the towering Bat males. Tsunami approached her slowly and she remained still, trying to maintain her composure. Despite his unseeing eyes, she knew he was able to sense everything about her, and that knowledge alone was frightening.

"First night with our queen," he said with a teasing grin.

"Training starts at dawn, brethren," Snow said from his stance by the fire. "Let her get some rest."

One by one they walked past her to retire to their rooms. Unsure of where to go, Fly waited for someone to direct her. Vulkie was the last to pass by, motioning with his claw. "Come. Your room is at the end of the hall."

Fly couldn't help but stare up at him the entire time they walked together, fascinated by his scars and voice. He sounded much like a boy, but the depth of his speech was profound and gracious. There was a playful manner about Vulkie, a sense of wonderment, similar to what Fly herself felt when she was alone with Kiah.

"Two months with us," he said to her. "That's one month more than you had to bond with your husband."

"Should I be worried?"

Torches lined the hall as they moved forward, bits of firelight scattering and skipping around the walls.

"Just keep your mind clear as you feel the physical changes. Breathe. It will be painful as you transform, but it is part of the process. Every female goes through the same thing as a child. Bat females," he said with a wide grin, "are a tough lot."

"I can trust you to help me?"

"Aye," Vulkie said with a nod. "But us trusting you, Fly, is a different matter. I want to believe you are with us, but until I see your dedication in full Bat form, I may also bear my doubts."

They stopped before the last door and Fly found herself afraid to enter the room alone. "I will do what needs to be done," she said to him.

Vulkie gently touched a claw to her cheek. "Good night."

As he started to turn around, Fly asked, "is there a Bat word for that?"

He winked at her over his shoulder. "Cladhnamiies, Queen Butterfly."

"Clath-nahm-ee-ehs," Fly echoed.

"Indeed," Vulkie nodded. He vanished into his room a few doors down, and Fly let herself into her own.

She looked around, noting that there were no windows to view the outside, no natural night streaming in, only four candles on a white wood nightstand across from the bed. On the bed lay new clothing for her.

"Here I stay alone," Fly whispered into the dark. "Without my beloved Kiah."

She moved the clothing off the bed and sat down, unwrapping her travel pack that Saedha had set on the floor. She took out the one thing she had brought with her from the cave. A special text from Kiah's ancient books. A text she had been forbidden to find. Songs from the Bat culture, including Ialchagor, the lullaby Kiah did not want her to learn.

"Ialchagor," Fly said quietly, as she sat up in bed. She followed the words on the page with her fingertips, pronouncing each syllable as it was written for a child Bat to learn.

Ialchagor's Lullaby
Ioah Aei Lirevh [eye-oh-ah ay leer-evh]
Aihmdi Doagh [ay-im-dee dew-age]
Araced Aei [ahr-ah-sed ay]
Nefiia Rahh [nee-fay-ah rah-ha]
Aosnn Aei [ah-sohn ay]
Eniridha [ehn-eer-ith-ah]
Eniridha [ehn-eer-ith-ah]

She repeated each sound to herself, humming her own tune,

imagining the voice of K'adhlenalde singing to her little Kiah. What did she sound like? Fly wondered. How did the Elf Bat queen sing?

13

Nightmares and Dancing

"Firestorm?"

The chill of the night has awoken the queen, Firestorm thought. He watched her enter the empty meeting room with her unruly curls, pale face, and trembling arms held tight to the cloak around her. She looked frightened.

"Can't sleep?"

She shook her head as she neared the hearth. The flames danced beneath their shadows on the wall, the darkness of the Sanctuary choking out signs of mirth. "I hear them cry. They cry in their sleep."

Firestorm turned to the hearth, gazing into the sparkling embers. "Who is it this time?" he asked in a hoarse voice.

"I don't know. So many rooms. Different sounds come from each door."

"Aye. The nightmares."

"Do they ever cease?"

"After twelve years, pretty girl, one thinks the terrible dreams would end. They do not."

Fly knelt on the stone floor, wrapping her blue cloak around her. "Is that why you are not sleeping?"

"No." Firestorm gave her a small smile. "I am just restless. Always liked to dance at night."

"Dance?"

"Each of us has a different story to tell. For me, Fly, the night of Banegildacht began with a celebration. I was seven years of age."

Fly smiled up at him, almost laughing. "I can't imagine any Bat dancing."

"Well now, you have much to learn yet of our culture, don't you?" He joined her on the floor as they both looked into the fire. "In a happier time, a time before Banegildacht, Elf Bats could create an entire dance celebration in Sidhovvn."

"No fooling, Fire?"

"No fooling. As a child I had a beautiful rhythm, and I had powerful wings to move with the drums." He touched his left shoulder. "They still are powerful. You've seen Kiah's, I assume?"

"I have," Fly said, eyes glowing in her growing fascination. "Did all Bat children go to these celebrations?"

"Only if they were friends with the host family's mother," Firestorm said with a chuckle. "But it was a triumphantly loud drumbeat that night. We were all lost in the music. Violins, giant drums set on boulder stands, fiddles. Then came the attack."

"You got away," Fly said. She leaned in as Firestorm's eyes darkened and his shoulders drooped. "How? What happened to you?"

"My dancing saved me that night. I can't tell you how I lasted the massacre without a scratch, but I can tell you that through the first minutes of the killing, I didn't even hear the swords or shrieks of my friends. I just continued to dance to the drums." He bit his bottom lip, averting his eyes from Fly. "I didn't know they were dying until the body of a nine-year-old friend whirled into me and shoved both of us onto the floor of the cave. I thought he had pushed me on purpose and I swung my fists into his chest to retaliate. But he was dead." Firestorm looked back at her. "And then I heard everything clearly. I saw. Bodies everywhere. Decapitated, wingless, strung up by chains. Fear. I felt nothing but fear."

"You got out."

"I crawled, slithered on my belly, kept as low as I could against the floor until I made my way to the moonlight. I didn't imagine I would fly home to find my own cave in the same state. My parents dead."

Fly remained silent for a long time, studying Firestorm's face, before staring into the fire as she said, "I'm glad you survived."

"I live with the same pain as the others. But it manifests in unique ways for us all." Firestorm got up to take the black cloak that lay on top of a chair at the table and flung it across his shoulders, fastening it with fumbling claws. "I dance to relieve my agony."

Fly smiled up at him. "What is this dance? Is it easy to learn?"

Firestorm held out one arm to her. "Come."

FLY

They danced in front of the hearth, Fly following Fire's soft-spoken directions as he properly positioned her legs with the aid of his wings.

"Turn like this, arms out, then come toward me."

"Do wings help?"

"They do. When you get yours, Fly, your world will change.

They will serve you in your new life as a Bat wife and queen."

Fly breathed softly, feeling Fire's wings encircle her the way Kiah's had during their playful painting. He danced, claws holding onto her wrists, gently pushing her away from him, drawing her back in, his wings unfurling like a sail in a seething storm.

"Follow. Eyes on me, Fly. Keep looking right at me. I go back, you come forward. Keep the rhythm."

His eyes were fierce, his grip light.

"These movements are meant to be fluid, symbolizing strength, power, and the act of sacrifice. There is a similar version of this that Bat couples do in the sky together. We call it Achtelaummi."

"Ahk-tel-ah-um-eye," Fly repeated.

"Good. It means 'unity flight'."

"Unity. Like the Bat word 'Ilumiaoacht'."

Fire grinned. "Ilumiaoacht, aye. Unified purity."

"Every word in the Bat language is beautiful."

"It is."

"Fire, I never danced with Kiah. He doesn't seem to be the dancing sort."

Fire's wings folded at his back as he twirled Fly and drew her close.

"All Bats can dance. He just needs to be reminded of the pleasures of wings mirroring a loved one. Trust me, Fly. When he comes home, the first thing Kiah will do is initiate the unity flight with you."

"But how will I know what to do?"

"That's why I'm teaching you now. This is the ground version."

Fly looked up at Fire as his claw moved from her back to her shoulders. They continued to move together in a slow rhythm.

"Is the dancing always this slow?" Fly asked.

"No. That is what the drums are for."

"Do you have any drums here?"

Fire stopped swaying, taking his claws off her. "I believe," he said, walking backward toward the front door, "it is time for such pleasures." He beckoned with his right claw. "Come. Come with me."

"Where?"

"Into the night."

Giant hollow drums were set against the exterior of the Sanctuary, the tops of them covered with leaves and dirt. The clearing just outside the door was large enough for multiple Bats to dance with unfurled wings. Fly heard shuffling and whispers inside the walls as Fire began tapping on the drums, and Vulkie, Tor, and Ty all emerged in grey bodysuits, cloaks draped around them.

"Initiating a dance without us, Fire?" Tor asked in an incredulous tone. "How terrible of you."

"It is worth mentioning, Tor, that I only wanted to show Fly a small taste of what a Bat dance is like."

"Not without my fiddle, you aren't," Soo said, joining them in the darkness. He withdrew the instrument from his cloak and pointed at Tor. "Drum with Fire. I'll show our queen proper Bat music."

Fly took a few steps back as Soo came forward, his blind eyes iridescent in the moonlight.

"The purpose of dancing is to unify a people together. If we cannot embrace each other in the coldness of the world, why bother living at all? We need to touch, to feel, to know our loved ones are safe from shadow."

"Is the dance Fire showed me meant for couples?"

"It was created for group celebrations, dearest. Even among Bat children. We all learn this dance by the age of three."

"I get to hear you play, Master Soo?"

"Aye." He touched the bow to the strings and set the darkness of the night alight with music.

SNOWBLIND

Fly circled backward, away from Snowblind, as he came outside with Caine and Vale. Snowblind saw a fearful respect in her eyes.

"Who initiated this?" he asked gruffly, looking around at the other Bats.

"Forgive us, Snow," Fire said, "but I thought you were too old for such an indulgence."

"I am only forty-seven years, son," Snowblind said, brows furrowed as he walked up to Fire standing behind the drums. "What makes you think I cannot dance?"

Vulkie went to Fly, gripping her arm and pulling her into the middle of the clearing. "I still want to dance with Fly. She never had a proper Bat wedding reception."

"Back yourself out of the clearing, Volcano," Snowblind said in a stern voice. He shrugged off his cloak and opened his wings. "The girl can watch."

Tor traded smirks with Ty as they stood with their wings out, flanking Soo. "What brought you out here, Snow? Was it the drums or the fiddle?"

Snowblind lifted a claw and motioned for Fire to start drumming again. He pointed his other claw at Soo. "Tsunami," he said, "strings."

"So?" Tor shouted above the music. "Which was it?"

Snowblind started dancing, his wings propelling him up into elaborate spins and flips in the air. The chill of the night renewed his weary mind.

"The fiddle," he called out, while flapping his wings in the sky, "is infectious. Drums are for finding one's rhythm. The fiddle is for flying in it."

Snowblind could see Fly watching him from the ground, eyes wide, delicate mouth slightly open, her mind and heart racing as she stood transfixed by the beauty of his wings.

To trust a purebred would be deadly, Snowblind thought. He could not give her his life...no matter how deeply she longed to be one of the winged brethren.

"Keep it going!" Vulkie shouted gleefully to Fire and Soo. He spun and dipped Fly, trying to get her to focus on mirroring him. But Fly was still looking up. She didn't take her eyes off Snowblind.

"I'm going to fly like that?"

Vulkie followed her eyes. "Aye. Soon you will, lovie. You'll be flying with all of us."

They danced until their wings and limbs drooped with exhaustion, each one retiring back to their rooms for sleep.

If you could have seen me dance, Snowblind wrote in his notebook. *If you could dance with me one more time, my love.*

14

The Teaching

"Who wants to bet me that she will shriek when she sees herself in the mirror?"

"That's not funny, lad."

"Me. I'll take it," Ty said, raising a coffee-filled tankard. "She will shriek."

"I say she won't," Vale said. "She isn't as loud as you, Vulkie."

They waited, doing their best to mind their own business as they heard Fly come down the hall and near the full-length mirror that stood just before the arch of the meeting room. Ty's mouth was full of hot coffee as he whipped his head from Vulkie to Vale and then back at Snow who sat at the table reading. Snow turned a page, glancing up as he also prepared to see Fly's reaction.

The sound that came from her mouth made all of them jolt. Vulkie traded a wing-five with Ty as they noticed bits of dirt crumble from the ceiling above them.

"I told you," Vulkie hissed at Vale. "Fly?" He composed himself before approaching her.

"Tell me this is normal." Fly's voice was shaking. "This is normal, isn't it?"

"Girl," Snow said from behind his book, "it could not get any more normal. That was the finest female Bat shriek I've heard in my life." He winked and gave a secret half-smile to Vulkie and Ty, their expressions giddy.

"How painful is it going to get? Is blood supposed to be coming out of me?" Fly stared at her arms, hands, the tips of her fingers as she unsteadily walked to the table. She pressed her palms lightly to her cheeks. "My face feels like tree bark." Sitting down, the tips of her claws scraped the table's surface and she drew them back, hugging herself.

"Take a breath," Vulkie said as he brought a plate of bread and sat next to her. "Breathe. Breathe like normal. Let your mind adjust to your body."

FLY

The lengths of her fingers burned as she tried to grasp the teacup before her. The claws splitting out of her fingertips felt like enduring splinters, creeping further by the hour. Emerging fangs cut into her gums and siphoned the moisture from her lips, causing them to crack. Her cheeks and hairline were dry, and the skin from her neck down had grown callous in the night.

"Here." Ty placed a tankard in front of her and slid the teacup away. "Coffee. Tor and I use it as our source of strength. Tea's too weak for us, and this cup is bigger."

"Thank you." Fly lowered her head, curls cascading around her face as she sipped at it without picking it up in her ungainly developing claws. Steam swirled into her eyes and she sputtered. "Everything's blurry. I can't see straight."

"Your eyes are darkening," Snow said, sounding pleased to

share the bad news. "They will reset into new colors for your Bat irises. The blurred, double vision is temporary, but the weakening of your sight is not. Your hearing will sharpen with the loss of strength in your eyes."

Vulkie chewed a piece of bread as he opened his mouth to speak. "At least you didn't wake up with eight extra spiked limbs protruding from your body."

Fly turned her head, watching him wiggle his claws at her. "Eight limbs?"

"I was rescued on Banegildacht by an eight-legged creature. A Spitxz."

"A what?"

"You never heard of those? They are a legendary underground people." He breathed right onto her face and repeated, "Spitxz, as in the word 'spit'." He spat onto the floor for emphasis. A dribble of saliva glistened between his terribly crowded fangs. "Crossbreed of spider, man, and goblin. Lovely family but terrifying bedtime stories," he said with a shudder.

Ty slid over to sit on the other side of Fly. He tilted his head toward her still steaming mug of coffee. "How do you like it?"

"It is strong," Fly said, gingerly cradling it between her palms.

"Here. Relax your wrists." Ty took the tankard from her. "I know the claws don't feel natural, but you have to learn to grasp things with them. They will be growing much longer. Adapt." He held his right claw in front her. "Adapt to this."

Fly raised her left hand, extending her pointer finger to touch the edge of his claw. She trembled as she tried to steady herself, fear welling as she felt the hard claw in her own hand brush against Ty's.

"It's all right. Feel the tip of my claw with yours."

She breathed out, pushing the dense, grey bit of Bat claw into his. The sound of two Bat claws connecting was no different than the sound of rock against rock. It astounded and frightened Fly.

"That's it." Ty smiled at her and she weakly smiled back, bringing herself to grasp the tankard of coffee.

"I'd say it's time for a proper Bat lesson." Vulkie bounced into the chair across from Fly and waved Saedha over. "Lavender pudding," he said as the gobliness set two bowls down.

"Is it really?" Fly asked, her face lighting up.

"Aye. We heard it's your favorite. But before eating, lovie, I have to teach you the Bat way of consuming food."

Fly frowned. "I already know how to make a mess of my meals."

Vulkie wagged his head. "It's not about the sloppiness. The technique itself matters." He dropped his face into the bowl, eating his pudding in an even wilder manner than she had gotten used to seeing with Kiah.

"Don't teach her that," Ty said.

Vulkie lifted his head, drawing in a deep breath and coughing out spurts of purple. "I have to. It's so she can pass it on to her future children."

Fly's eyes widened at his words and he cocked his head innocently. "What? Your marriage to Kiah gives us hope for an heir."

"That's enough of breakfast." Snow's voice boomed, startling Vulkie out of the banter he was clearly enjoying. "Fly, come outside with us."

"I need to change my clothes."

"A white bodysuit is waiting on your bed."

"White? Are you certain I won't be getting it filthy?"

Snow gave her a hard look, as if she were a disagreeable child.

"What does it matter, girl? Should you end up in the dirt during your training you will look more like a warrior. Go change. We will be outside."

Fly retreated to her room, finding the bodysuit laid on top of the bed. It had a higher collar than the other suits she had worn in Kiah's cave, the form-fitting style and rigid collar matching the bodysuits of the eight male Bats.

SNOWBLIND

"Who's going to teach her the Bat shriek?" Vulkie asked excitedly as they all gathered outside the Sanctuary.

"Not you, Vulkie," Snowblind said with a terse shake of the head. "You are far too loud."

"My technique is perfect."

"It is not just screaming at the sky. It's the war cry. The shriek comes at the end of the word."

"What is your war cry?" Fly asked. She looked up at Snow-blind, eager for an answer.

"It is this." Snowblind prepared to whisper into Fly's ear, then seeing the excitement in Vulkie's eyes, decided against it.

"Tell me," Fly said. "Out loud. What is the war cry?"

Vulkie suddenly yelled the word and shrieked, causing the trees to quake and bend at their roots. Unapologetic, he shrugged at Snowblind's glare. "Traditionally, it's used within a legion of Bats. But since it's only a small attack against the king it won't sound quite as foreboding."

"So-bah-ork-aye-ehld?" Fly echoed in a gentle voice.

"Aye." Vulkie shrieked again, scattering birds from the trees. "Siobahorkeilde!" He grinned at her amusement.

Fly laughed, entranced by his boyish antics, and followed him toward the thick of the forest.

Snowblind shook his head as he watched, running his claws over his hair. "Caine, tell me there is a way to make the baby Bat less exuberant."

Caine chuckled, shifting his weight to his good leg. "Vulkie's spirit reminds me of my eldest brother. He drove my mother mad during mealtimes."

"Was he just as loud?"

"Aye. He was. But I would not discourage Vulkie, Snow. Fly needs a bit of joy before we all stand against the evil."

"Fair point. Butterfly, we have much to teach you," he called out. "Come now."

Seeing her sprint out from the trees with a joyful countenance beside the equally carefree Vulkie, Snowblind felt an ache in his chest. *Our queen looks so much like you, Meaghiea,* he thought. *So much like you, my daughter. And so much like your mama.*

FLY

"Fly, you will be running with Caine across the tops of the trees. Let us see how light and quick you are."

"Yes, Master Snow."

"Go on, girl. Go."

Without further word from Snow, Fly ran alongside Caine, surprised at the one-legged Bat's speed. He flew to the treetops as she made the climb up into the branches.

"Quick, Fly!" Snow shouted at her. "The Bloodmanghe will be behind you. Be quick."

She reached the top, crouching low as the leaves rustled in the wind around her.

"Where's your reckless spirit, beauty? Come now and catch me." Caine laughed as he ran backward, wings folded at his back. "I won't cheat with my wings if you keep pace. Come,

come."

"How do you fare so well?" Fly asked. "You only have a single leg and a single arm, yet you run like a stallion."

"Adaptation is key to strength. Adapt, beauty. Listen to your pulse, your breath, your heart. Run into the wind."

"Why do I tire so fast? I should not."

"Your body's changes, Fly," Caine said as moved backward. "The Bat in you is creating fatigue in your purebred muscle. Fight it. Adapt. You must push on."

Fly glanced down. "How far do we go?"

"Entire forest. This is a test for you. Follow."

The sky was clear around them. Fly could see the sun and shadows it created against rock and living things below. She faltered in her step, balancing herself on a tight cluster of leaves.

"Kiah taught me how to call the bats."

Caine stood a few feet from her, looking out at the sun. He took a crumb of tough bread from within his suit's pocket and chewed it slow. "Aye? Show me."

Fly drew a breath, raising her face and arms to the sky. She shrieked as loud and long as she could. Caine lifted his head as brown and black bats came from every direction, each one acknowledging him with a short chirp as they circled.

"Natural call, beauty," he said with a smile.

"Aye," Fly nodded. "They're beautiful."

"You have so much wonder in your heart, dear Fly," Caine said. "You were born to be a Bat."

SNOWBLIND

"What do you really think of her, Snow?"

"She is playful and gentle. But she is not as strong as our Bat females were."

"She will be. She is transforming," Vale said. "You must believe in her."

Snowblind crossed the floor of the Sanctuary's library. He felt Vale's fondness for Fly and for his hope of survival.

"Your encouragement is not enough. The Bloodmanghe will not die with one strike or two. It will be many swings of a blade and many pieces of pyro-cannon dropped from the sky. We will not make it without the unbreakable force of a Bat queen and king."

"Kiah is coming back. He will see her strong. They will fight together, Snow. And they will defend us."

For our families, Snowblind thought. *We must honor the dead.*

We will make it, Vale said in his mind. *No fear, Snow. Do not fall to fear.*

FLY

At the noon hour, Tor and Ty led Fly to the river clearing and pointed toward the rocks jutting out of the water. "See there, Fly. You must maintain your balance while we fire arrows at you."

"What sort of test is this?"

"Reflex." Ty drew an arrow from his pack and casually snapped it in half. "Don't worry. They will be blunt."

"You wish to see me dance upon the rocks of the river?"

"Exactly." Tor grinned at Ty and they both fitted new arrows to their bows. "Step out."

Fly noticed Tor's rugged, ebony hair shine in the sunlight as he trained his weapon on her. He maintained a jovial face, completely engrossed and amused by what he was preparing to do.

"Are you serious?" Fly asked. She started to laugh, halting

herself when she saw their smiles fade.

"Step out," they said in unison. "Show your balance, little queen."

"Right then. I'll show you."

Fly gingerly stepped from land to the haphazard path of wet river rocks, positioning herself on a smooth boulder in the middle of the flowing water. Just as she turned to face the Bats, Tor fired the first arrow.

"Agility," Ty called out to her as she ducked. "Bend with the wind."

She spun and skipped from one slippery rock to the next, bending backward as they rained arrows around her. Her flexibility and speed impressed them until she suddenly looked up, distracted by Vulkie's airborne somersaults, while both of her feet were planted on separate river rocks.

"Kill shot!" Tor shouted before releasing an arrow. At the arrow's impact, Fly fell backward into the water, and the Bats tried to muffle their laughter.

"I blame the wings," Fly muttered as she swam to the river's edge. "It is fascinating to see a Bat fly."

Ty cocked his head as he returned his remaining arrows to his quiver. "You're easily distracted, beauty. That may be your undoing."

15

Hidden

"It is nightfall, Fly," Vale said at dinner. "I'm taking you out for your next lesson."

"Where are we going?"

"Deep into the forest. The core of it, where it is darkest."

Fly noticed Ty and Tor snickering at the other end of the table, and at her curious look, they immediately ceased. "Forgive us, beauty," Tor said. "I can't imagine you will bode well in pitch black darkness."

"Nothing to laugh at, Tor," Soo said between loud slurps of stew. "I adapted to my loss, she will adapt to hers."

"I was not poking fun at your situation, Tsunami. I only know from witnessing the behavior of purebred Elves, that most do not thrive in the dark."

Vale, rising from the table, shook his head. "Come, Fly. Leave them to their jesting."

The quiet of the forest heightened Fly's sense of the Bat transformation in her body. She tried to stifle pained groans as she followed Vale through the trees. Each one seemed more connected to the next, the twisting of branches and trunks making one rely on scampering and vaulting to make it to the center of the trunks. The darkness surpassed any cave.

"You can't even see the stars anymore," Fly said, head tilted back.

Vale gave her a knowing look despite their limited sight in the night, sensing her questions about Soo. "Soo lost his sight when he tried to save his baby sister from the Bloodmanghe, but the majority of Elf Bats do not go fully blind."

Fly felt heat rise to her cheeks, reminded yet again that her mind was not the private place it had once been. "Master Tsunami did not tell me of that."

"One day you will know all of our stories, Fly."

"So, we do not lose sight completely, but it does deteriorate?"

"Aye. Your eyes are weakening. This is when it is time for you to rely on your other senses. Hearing is the most crucial when taking to the sky."

Fly admired Vale's placid demeanor as he spoke with her. Each Bat carried himself in a stark individuality, yet they stood unified as one people.

"How many Bats were here before Banegildacht?"

"Thousands. You could pick any one point in the clouds and a parent Bat would dive out with their young. The sky would be filled with families in the midst of courage dives and playing together. Wings unfurled and the happiest of shrieks mixed with the wild bats." Vale looked up at the ceiling of leaves. "It was a sight, my dear. If not for that night, I would be up there dancing with my Beryl."

"Beryl? Was she a Bat too?"

"Aye. Listen to the silence, Fly. Feel the trees with your claw tips, sense the direction of the breeze with your ears."

"How old was she?" Fly asked as she laid her palms against a rough tree trunk. She could see nothing, not even her own arms as she held them out in front of her. Vale stood across from her, only his eyes visible.

"You must have met as children."

"We did. We were playing a game of Bat tag with a group of friends that night in the forest. I was twelve, she was thirteen. I had been trying to overcome my shyness to tell her I wanted her to be my mate when I turned eighteen."

"Bat tag?"

Vale chuckled in the dark. "I knew you would be intrigued by that. I will show you at another time."

"The Bloodmanghe attacked you then?"

"Aye. We had no idea of what was happening around us. The trees were near as thick and dark as these are. At only thirteen years, a female Bat's wings are still weak. She could not fly as high or as fast as me. I did what I could to save her. Both of us fought for our lives. But they knocked me out and I woke up alone in a field. Her body was gone."

"And you knew she was dead?"

"I had no other choice than to believe it. I flew home to find my own family slaughtered. A Bat cave without a family is nothing but fear and chill."

Fly could tell Vale wanted to divert his attention to a lighter subject when he bluntly asked her, "did you ever love before Kiah?"

"I did not."

"No one ever before that you fancied? Not even the slightest bit of adoration?"

"Most of the males my age were told to stay away from me in the city. The king wanted me at his constant beckoning and my father never wanted me to leave the house except for work."

"Ah." Vale grinned in the dark, flashing his top fangs. "So you were King Averee's secret love pet."

"I was not!" Fly snapped, spine tingling at the thought.

"It sounds like it, my dear. He had you on a leash. Did he often stare when you were in his court?"

"Sometimes, yes. But he did not seek my affections."

"And did he tell you what to wear?"

"Daily, yes. But it was his choice of clothing fitted to my service in his court. I never chose."

"That, my dearest, is a love pet." Vale came close, breathing on her hair, towering over her. "He would've dishonored you had he gotten you alone."

"You mean," Fly said, voice trembling, "violated me."

"Aye."

"I cannot imagine him attacking me in that way."

"And yet, Fly, you are here with us because you believe that he violated and killed our Bat females."

"I am here because I value life the same as you, Master."

He took a step back, claws clasped behind his back. "Good. But I offer a warning, Fly." The warmth disappeared from his voice, his face suddenly serious. "Do not let any one of us tempt you to break Kiah's trust."

"W-what?" Fly flinched at his words, her previous state of calm shaken.

"Just because we are choosing celibacy," Vale said, turning from her as he started back toward the Sanctuary, "does not mean we don't feel desire."

In the echo of Vale's ominous words, Fly resisted sleep that night. She sought comfort in ancient texts and, with the help of Saedha the gobliness, found the Sanctuary's hidden library. As she took in the sight of the thousands of books lining the walls from floor to ceiling, Fly saw she was not the only one looking for peace.

SNOWBLIND

"And on this night, we shall not die quiet. We shall not bow to cowardice." Snowblind paced as he read from the pages he held, glasses repeatedly sliding down his nose every time he pushed them back up. "We are Bats of Jekkiliah. Brethren to the wing and fang. Defending all life, sacred pleasures, the purities in this world. Defending it forever. Defending it—" He paused in his pacing and read the last three words in a whisper, head bowed. "To our end."

"You glisten in the candlelight."

He raised his head to see Fly watching him, her curly-haired head tilted as she stared at his bare back and shoulders, the trickles of sweat covering his body. She was probably studying the four tattoos on his left shoulder.

"I sweat during my night terrors." He tried not to sound agitated by her presence. "I can barely breathe lying down and trying to sleep upside down is even worse."

Fly said nothing. She came forward, crouching to peruse the shelves of books.

Snowblind tore the glasses off his nose and tossed them aside. He slammed his book closed. "How did you find this place?"

"Is there no door?"

"Not one that is easily spotted, my girl."

The look on Fly's face confused him. She appeared both teasing and solemn.

"I asked Saedha if she had any books in the Sanctuary," Fly said. "She directed me to this room."

"Ah." Snowblind rolled his eyes as he looked away from her. "Of course."

"Are Elf Bats nocturnal like the animal?"

He answered while perusing a section of bookshelves, the white book of poetry still in his claw. "We do draw our strength from the night. But since Banegildacht, we find no rest in day or night. The price of years-long grief has destroyed our natural sleep pattern."

"So, you would fly all night if you had the energy."

"Aye."

"Why don't you go out now instead of restlessly pacing in here?"

Snowblind sighed and uttered a growl. Fly's questions were relentless. "I am preparing my body to do so. Only when Kiah comes back, will any one of us take to the sky in the dark."

"You flew around at night during Fire's drumming."

"Music soothes. Music gives me courage. Poetry does the same."

"Are there many texts here about battle?"

"The history of battle or a tale of outright bloodshed? You know, Fly, I have lived both."

She picked a book out of a shelf and flipped through it. "Swords. I have to learn."

"In due time," Snowblind said. He strode to her and tore the book from her hands. "A duel with a blade is not about the bloodshed or release of anger. For a Bat, it is the tipping point, the means to defend one's honor and the honor of the fallen."

Fly did not look offended by his harsh gesture. "To obtain justice," she agreed.

"Not only justice. Balance between the two who fight. I do not wish to take the life of a count, but in the act of righting the violence against my family, I will do so."

Fly saw the gap widen between them as Snowblind circled away from her, holding the book up high as an imaginary sword.

"You don't trust me," she said.

He bared his fangs. "Why should I? Your parents, even if not your blood, slaughtered my family."

"They followed orders. I have no part in their darkness."

"You cannot be greater than Queen K'adhlenalde."

"It is not my intent, Master Snow." Fly kept her eyes on him, moving backward, mirroring his movements. "I am beneath your strength."

"I wish you could have seen my wife Adreinnha. She would have told me if you are as worthy as Kiah believes you are."

"I do not learn to be worthy, Master. I want to defend you. I want to defend the Elf Bats."

"You do not know the sight or sound of death. You do not know it. The servants of the king deserve death. They deserve pain."

"Consequence." Fly breathed softly.

"Aye," Snowblind said, bowing his head. "Protection of the honor of females who I failed that night."

"Their deaths aren't on you."

"I should've been home."

"Then you would be dead too."

"I live to fight." They stood across from each other, several feet apart, Snowblind still raising the book over his head.

"I'm not against revenge," Fly said, pulling her shoulders back. "I will fight for you."

"Good."

"But I don't think Kiah carries the same anger as you."

"He harbors and manifests it differently. I know he has had

violent outbursts."

"None that I can't handle, Master."

Snowblind drew close, whispering into the dim room. "You don't know how deep the pain goes, Fly. It's beyond healing."

16

Twin Blades

TSUNAMI

"A few days of agility training may not satisfy Snow," Tsunami said. "But from what I read of your body, dearest, you are now ready to handle a blade."

"Is this room built for weapons?"

"Aye. Not used often, but now, in our time of need, it is key to your training."

Tsunami knew when he was being watched. Fly marveled at him, a searching air in her cautious breaths. She seemed to hold him in a high regard, a regard not given to just any living creature in her world.

"Vale told you about Autmhae," he said.

"What?"

"My baby sister. You are thinking of her as you look at me, aren't you? She was three months old on the night of her death."

"I'm so sorry, Master."

"I am not a master of anything but my own grief. You need not carry on with formalities for the sake of respect."

"But it is respect. You are worthy of it, Soo."

"I took her out of the cradle and ran with her in my arms. I remember running to the back of our cave where there was a way down, but there was no soft landing for us. I tried to fly. Bloodmanghe came from all sides, prying Autmhae from my arms and striking the back of my head."

"How did they blind you?"

"Later they dragged me across the floor to watch my father be tortured. He was chained tight to his own bed. Blood, shrieks, bits of shredded wing, all of it strewn in front of my eyes. And then came the light. The fire. I saw nothing more." He gripped the hilts of the twin blades, lifting them from their platform for Fly to see. "Nothing ever again."

Fly's footsteps were soft against the floor. She had backed away from him.

"These are the blades of the Bats. Have you held a sword before, Fly?".

"Once. My father's."

"We wear these strapped to our backs beneath our wings during battle. You draw them out like this." He held out the blades for her to take, and feeling her firmly grasp them, he demonstrated with an agile unsheathing of his own blades.

"Twin blades."

"Aye."

"Not swords," Fly said. "Knives."

"We call them short swords as they are more compact for easy carry and dual wielding. But indeed, they are made for battle."

He listened to the ring of metal as Fly steadily ran the tips of her claws along the edges.

Tsunami grinned, sensing her cautious excitement. "When a Bat's wings and blades work in tandem, the accuracy is perfection."

"Are these mine?"

"Aye. Designed for you to carry and wield in our attack, Fly. You will practice."

His cloudy eyes shifted down and to the left, body turning as Snow entered the room behind him.

"Showing her the weapons already, Soo?"

"Anything to strengthen her knowledge."

"It is not yet time for the duel training," Snow said.

"I'd say she is ready."

They both looked in Fly's direction. "Would you like to try, dearest?"

"Who do I fight?" Fly asked.

Tsunami traded sly grins with Snow.

FLY

"You'll notice, Fly, that despite full length claws, we can all wield bows and blades. It is both an instinctive and learned technique in which the center of each weapon is stabilized between palm and thumb. We can grasp blades as you see Soo doing, as our claws are made to flex. But you can't rely on arm strength alone. Unfurled wings always give us an advantage when joined with the arrow or blade."

Fly held her blades against her chest as she circled backward.

"Uncross them. Timidity invites danger."

"You can hear my steps, can't you?" Fly said. "Even if I tried to be lighter, you could always sense my shadow."

"Your talking makes it easier for him to find you. Cease your voice, Fly," Snow said.

Fly watched Soo return his twin blades to his back, drawing out a different set.

"Hook swords?" she asked, noticing the different shape of

metal.

"He always fancies an extra set of blades." Snow sipped a cup of tea as they dueled around him in the room. "These will follow him into battle."

Fly looked confused as Soo backed away from her and crouched into a Bat crawl, blades still in his claws.

"What are you doing? Is that a tactic for surprising the enemy?"

"When a Bat lays a trap, dearest," Soo said, "every position is vital to the success of the capture. Sometimes we make a game of it before delivering the final blow."

"He likes to play with his prey before consuming it," Snow said with a chuckle.

"You confuse them," Fly said. "Is that what you mean?"

"A diversion, distraction, or even faking a mortal wound. Once they come back around, you spring on them. And you must do it silently."

Snow circled backward, motioning for Fly to engage Soo with her blades.

"Pay mind to your own weakness, Fly, and you will find it to be your greatest strength."

"I don't know my weakness." Fly ducked under Soo's hard swing.

"Your love of questions, your love of chatter," Snow said. "You can use it to both irritate and distract in the midst of a duel."

"Hardly a distraction," Soo said. "Snow, that is terrible advice."

"Why?"

"When she fights me, I can hear everything. The tiniest word from her mouth would be a death sentence if I meant her harm."

Fly heard Snow chuckling behind her. "Are you trying to make me stumble, Master Snow?"

"No. I'm amusing myself just watching you two. And if the Bloodmanghe were dimwits, surely your constant chatter would give them pause in battle."

"Oh, Snowblind," Soo said in exasperation, "you sound like a fool."

"Tell me," Fly asked, "would my greatest weakness work on the king?"

"If King Averee is as feeble as he claims, you would only need one measure to slay him."

Fly halted her blades, holding them in the air. "What is that?"

She suddenly hit the floor, Soo tripping her up with the hook edge of his blades. Snow stood over her and smiled as she realized what had happened.

"All you need, girl," Snow said, extending his claw, "is a Tsunami."

"It pays to have two sets of swords. One for the capture," Soo quickly sheathed the hook blades and drew out the standard twin blades. "And one for the final kill."

Fly looked up at him.

"Are you smiling or glowering, dearest?" Soo asked.

"Neither. I'm astounded by your tactic. And speed. You are very fast with a blade. But the Bloodmanghe are not quick on their feet. You should know that about them."

"It matters not how quick they are," Snow said. "If you don't stay upright in the battle, you will be dead either way."

"Do I ever throw a sword?"

"Never. Why would you unhand the only thing between you and a stab to the heart?"

Fly grinned, running backward as Soo lunged toward her

with his blades. "I think Vulkie would throw swords at the Bloodmanghe."

"No. He has his own methods. Throwing your blade into the air for a trick is not going to keep you alive, nor will it impress a broadly built Bloodmanghe."

"So," Fly said with a pout, "I can't do anything fancy?"

"You do what you must to avoid the tip of a blade or arrow, Fly. You run from them if you have to. But when you are staring one down, you must engage with the utmost confidence." Snow placed his cup down on the stone table in the corner of the room. "A Bloodmanghe, like the one who took the life of Kiah's mother, will not think of you as innocent. They will only see us as targets to execute."

"Monsters of the underworld," Fly said, losing her breath for a moment as she somersaulted.

"Aye."

"But they are the monsters. They kill without question."

"Because they were ordered to. The king personally chose all of them to defend his city and to carry out any means of violence toward his people."

"We are not his people," Fly said. She popped back up, swinging at Soo, driving him back toward the wall. He grinned as he blocked her, sensing her confidence.

"Aye. Which is why he hates us the most."

"But Bats are not violent. Bats protect the innocent."

"Bats also defend the honor of the fallen. Like little Autmhae and my father." Soo halted Fly in her pacing, touching the point of his right blade to her neck. "When I face Count Llieghonu there will be no mercy. He will know my wrath."

"You kill for your dead," Fly said.

"Aye. That we do. Only those who spilled Bat blood on their

hands."

"Averee did not. He avoided being near the killing."

"The hand that penned Banegildacht is the most wicked. He will suffer by other means."

"Meaning?" Fly asked.

"I will not have the honor of seeing the king fall. I only look to Count Llieghonu and the Blooodmanghe."

"Who will go for the king?" Fly turned her head from the tip of Soo's blade as he continued to hold it out.

Snow approached them. "I have a thought, Fly, that it is you and Kiah who will be tending to him."

Suddenly Soo crossed his blades and Fly fumbled before mirroring him with hers.

"Now what?" she asked. "What do I do?"

"Increase the difficulty, girl," Snow said to her. "Come."

The Bats led her out from the weapons room to the clearing in front of the Sanctuary.

"A different sort of practice," Soo said with a crooked grin.

"Odds are that you will be battling more than one Blood-manghe at a time. Maybe even four. But for our purposes, we will only have you fight two. Caine!" Snow called out.

Caine charged from out of the trees toward Fly and Soo. Fly took to a defensive stance, using every bit of mental strength to anticipate where her blades would go and how swiftly they would swing. This time the fight was not as forgiving. Fly felt the tremble in her muscles as she gripped her blades tight amidst the blows, forcing herself to imagine that Caine and Soo were not friends, but Bloodmanghe. And in the way of the Bats, she had to breathe in the scent of metal against wind and listen close to the ring of blades.

VULKIE

Vulkie took an hour to sharpen his balance on the river rocks, watching Fly learn of every Bat's secret weapon. She was positioned on the edge of the water with Fire and Vale as they explained the hard material in their palms.

"The appearance is of an ilmenite rock, but the texture is of pumice. It comes in all sizes and generally we have it stashed in a pack slung across our backs."

"Pyro-cannon?" Fly asked. She held out her claw to take the piece they handed to her.

"Pyro-cannon is an explosive element, a rock, used to disorient and deflect enemy hits," Fire said.

"These are not deadly, nor are they to replace your blades." Vale flung his pyro-cannon toward Vulkie, who immediately ducked. The rock exploded as it skipped across the water.

"It is meant to buy yourself more time, when you have none left."

"And," Fly asked, "what if you use up your supply?"

Fire crossed his arms over his chest, flicking two pieces of pyro-cannon into the trees where they briefly flashed against the rough trunks. "There will always be a Bat at your call. Shriek distress and we will come."

"Always," Vale agreed. "We got your back."

FLY

During a late night after dinner, Fly found herself alone with Caine at the table. They both appeared to be lost in thought, eating their lavender pudding by the light of the hearth.

"Why did you choose Kiah?" he asked her after several minutes of silence.

"I'm not sure I can explain."

"You're always blushing, little queen. What is it about us? What is it about Kiah that made you love him?"

"I never felt accepted in my own home in Adreachterum. I felt judged by the other purebreds. When I made the choice to run away with the king's book, I didn't know where I was running, but something pushed me to climb Ialchagor's cliff. Something unseen."

"Sounds like you never were a typical purebred," Caine said. His bottom fangs were stained purple from his pudding.

"Were your parents a typical Bat couple?"

"They were very much in love until the day their lives were stolen."

"Did you have any siblings?"

"Aye." He smiled. "I would do anything to defend them."

"Is that how you lost your arm and leg? You tried to shield them?"

"The count humored me. He encouraged me to fight the Bloodmanghe. Even as a child, I knew there would be consequences when I chose to defend my family on Banegildacht. I didn't know they would alter my life as much as they did, but I would not have chosen different."

Fly could see the emotion in his eyes. "Even though you didn't save them?"

"I showed my courage," Caine said. "Even in a losing battle, you should never reveal your weakness. Never."

17

The Heir

Soaking in cold water was the only source of relief for an itchy, scaly back. Tor told Fly as much when she emerged from her bedroom ferociously scratching at the rash spreading down her shoulders and back.

"Your skin is flaking and dry as bone. Bathe in the river, dear queen. We will give you privacy."

Fly journeyed to the river shortly before sunrise, Tor and Ty trailing behind her. She stood at the edge of the water and gazed down at her reflection.

Ty glanced over his shoulder and smiled. "Fly, may I have a gaze at your swim?"

"Face the trees, Bat," Fly said crossly. She growled in her struggle to undress and toss the clothing to the grass. Everything got caught on her claw tips.

"Aye, lass, aye." They raised one arm each as they stood with their backs turned. "We promise not to dishonor the queen. We stand guard, nothing more."

Despite the difference in Tor's choppy ebony hair and Ty's

haphazard bun at the nape of his neck, they looked the same to Fly. All of the Bats had the same height of eight feet, but their builds were varied, some more bony or muscular than others.

"Am I going to get taller?" Fly asked from the water.

"No. You will stay at your six-foot height."

"Why don't I grow in my Bat transformation?"

"Don't gripe, Fly," Ty said. "You are getting everything else. Some things cannot be explained."

"I don't mind having to look up at you, but it'd be nice to gain a few inches."

"You will be a fine she-bat just as you are."

"Why make conversation, beauty, when you are immersed in water?" Tor asked, back still turned.

"You look like twins standing there. If you are not related, perhaps you grew up together in a shared cave."

"We did," Tor said in a surprised voice. "How did you know about the shared Bat caves?"

"I didn't. I only assume because of your similarities."

"Our families were in a community cave, aye. Multiple passages connected us, but we had separate living rooms."

"Did you have siblings?" Fly asked them.

"Only child," Ty answered. "My father locked me in our weapons closet to keep me safe that night. I heard everything outside the door. The Bloodmanghe never came for me."

"What about you, Master Tor? Did you come from a big family?"

"Three brothers. My mother had curly hair like yours, Fly. I watched Bloodmanghe pin her down and tear her curls from her scalp. The count bound her with ship's rope and committed the violation in front of me and my brothers. Two of my brothers came forward to stop him, and the Bloodmanghe grabbed each of us by the throat—"

"Excuse you, Bat," Ty loudly interrupted Tor. "What a terrible image to put in Queen Butterfly's head."

"I'm just telling her what happened. Of course it is terrible."

Fly submerged herself in the river to stifle a giggle, then came back up and breathed out slow.

"She will know the pain without you giving her nightmares, Tor. Let her relax."

"I'm not offended," Fly said as she swam toward the edge. "Could one of you toss me my clothes, please?"

They traded teasing looks and flung the garments over their shoulders toward the river, keeping their eyes straight ahead.

"Anything else, beauty?"

"No. I'm ready to go back. I'm hungry."

VULKIE

"Fly," Vulkie said later at breakfast, "race me to the bottom of the bowl."

Fly proceeded to consume three bowls of porridge alongside Vulkie, the others looking on with entertained eyes.

Fire smirked. "You eat more than any of us, Fly."

"She eats enough for two of her," Caine said.

"Maybe she's carrying a child," Vale piped up, face half covered by his tankard of coffee.

Fly's eyes widened and her bowl clattered onto the table. She sprung up in a rush and made a shallow bow, cheeks pink. "I need to get something from my room."

Vulkie watched her clumsily walk down the hall, her small frame careening from one side to the other like she was at sea, and suddenly she sprinted to the furthest door at the Sanctuary. He waited a few moments before standing and taking his leave from the table.

"I would not follow Fly," Caine called after him.

Vulkie halted and gave a look over his shoulder. "I need to see that she is all right. She has never left the table so fast."

"Son," Snow said, "give the girl her space."

"You don't sense trouble in Fly?"

"I do sense that something is not quite right, but I would not ask."

With his back turned, Vulkie shrugged and continued down the hall.

He found Fly sitting in her bedroom, arms clutched to her chest, body trembling. He heard a quivering breath from her mouth as she stared at the floor.

"Why did you flee like that, lovie?"

Fly's head whipped up at his voice.

"I had to find Saedha...to speak to her. I thought another female would understand."

"Understand what?"

Fly bit her lip, eyes welling with tears. "I was thinking about what Caine said. About me eating enough for two."

"Not a bad thing," Vulkie said with a slight smile. "Female Bats are known to have voracious appetites."

"It's more, Vulkie," she said.

Vulkie sat at the edge of the bed, lowering his voice as he sensed her fear. "What's wrong?"

"Kiah and I...we hadn't spoken of children, but I knew it was possible after the wedding night." Fly ceased speaking and just stared into his eyes.

Vulkie's mouth dropped. "You carry Kiah's heir."

"I do."

"That is the best news, lovie." He embraced her, his earrings jingling as he bounced in excitement. "The best news any of us could hear."

"Don't tell them. Don't tell Kiah." Fly drew back, wiping tears from her face. "Don't say anything to them."

"What? What is it?"

"I have to protect all of you in battle. Now I have to protect my own baby too. I won't be able to fight."

"Bat females are strong." Vulkie pulled her in for a tighter embrace. "You will fly with us no matter what."

"Kiah wouldn't allow it. He wouldn't want his son or his son's mama in harm's way."

Vulkie smiled. "It's a male?"

"Saedha told me." Fly withdrew from him, rising up to stand in the doorway. "She said a gobliness always knows."

"I won't tell anyone." Vulkie stood, eyes glowing. "Don't fear, Butterfly. We got your back."

"I trust you," Fly said.

"But you should know," Vulkie added, "I'm terrible at keeping secrets. You may have to lock me up until after Kiah returns."

Fly giggled. "I trust you. I trust all of you."

He looked down at her, awed by her acceptance and growth. "You are going to be a strong mama."

"I just want to be a good one."

"You will. Kiah is the luckiest Bat out of us all. He has you, Fly."

"He's going to be a father," Fly said, her expression softening.

"Aye. A very proud one."

"Vulkie," Fly said, stopping him as he headed back down the hall. "Will you help protect our heir?"

"I will. No evil will befall you, my queen, or your beloved."

Vulkie dropped to one knee and rested one of his claws on the top of her hand. "Your baby is safe. No more Bats are going to die. No more children sacrificed."

"You were the youngest that night," Fly said. "Banegildacht. Only four years old."

"Aye, I was."

"Do you remember anything?"

"I can still smell the ash and flame at night. And the shrieks of my mother. I always hear them in my dreams."

"Do you remember your father?"

Vulkie grinned. "Da was known among the Bats as a proper warrior. I only learned of his actions later from Vale and Snow. I never see much of him in my dreams."

"And..." Fly took a breath, hesitating to speak.

He saw her staring at the scars that covered his head and face, save for the sole section of long hair.

"Do you remember the pain?"

"Not as vividly as I used to. But I can feel it when I am near flame."

"I hope," Fly said earnestly, "you never face flame again."

18

Courage Dive

Fly opened her eyes on a morning of her second month at the Sanctuary, only to find herself rolled off of her bed, arms and legs sprawled, claws fully grown and digging into the floor. She tried to blow the straggling curls out of her eyes as she pushed up onto her knees, failing to get to her feet. She felt a weight at her back that had not been there before, a thick blanket of leather and skin beneath her tunic.

She crawled, trying to grasp the doorway with her claws. Every attempt to stand brought her back onto the floor. She could not lift her body.

"Masters! Masters, help me get up!" she called out. "I can't...
"

Soo came running down the hall, hearing her cries from the meeting room. He dropped to his knees and crawled next to her. "Dearest," he breathed in amazement, "you have your wings. Your wings want to carry you."

"Help me, Soo," Fly cried. She fought to grip onto the ground, claws scrabbling.

"You can get up. Butterfly, you can get up." Soo heard her moan as she tried to maneuver herself forward. "Come on."

"I can't. I can't do it."

"Come. Come on." Soo crawled alongside her. "Surrender control. Surrender your legs and your wings will lift you."

Fly emitted a primal, animalistic sound from her mouth as she finally pushed her body up, legs numb, head spinning, wrists burning.

"You have to think of your wings as a part of you. You are not a purebred Elf anymore, Fly." Soo smiled when she looked at him. He sounded full of pride. "You are a Bat. Believe you are a Bat."

Sweat matted the curls against her cheeks as Fly crawled, body aching as she struggled to use her wings for the first time. Through blurred eyes, she saw Snow encouraging her down the hall, beckoning to her with his claws.

"Good, Fly," Snow said to her. "Good girl. That's it. Come. Push forward. Come."

Fly felt like she had awoken in another creature's body and the terror of the sensation of wings at her back forced more moans of agony out of her mouth.

"Crawl, my love. Lift your wings to propel forward. Come."

"I can't...I can't..." Fly whimpered as she dragged herself barely an inch more across the floor. She tried to be conscious of her wings, tried to move them with her mind.

"My love, you must do this now," Soo said, "or you will never get up."

"Make the choice and commit to the act. Use your wings!" At Snowblind's stern yell, Fly released a high-pitched shriek and unlocked her arms, the edges of her wings finally thrusting forward against the ground and pushing her to stand. She gasped, shuddered, and lifted a hand to feel the thick, leathery appendages at her back.

"Yes," Snow said.

Fly looked directly into his eyes. He was nodding and smiling, his cracked top fangs gleaming. "Good girl."

Amidst hard breaths, Fly smiled back.

"She has her wings!" Soo joyously called out. He ran outside, charging past Vulkie and Fire who sat on the ground polishing their twin blades. They looked at him like he had lost his mind, before seeing Snow lead Fly out into the clearing.

"Come! Show her flight!"

The open space surrounding the Sanctuary was not as vast as the meadow beneath Ialchagor's Cliff and Fly didn't know how to take to the air as she ran, flanked by four of the Bats.

"Vulkie," Soo ordered, "guide her to a break in the treetops and get her up."

"Hold on to me, Fly." Vulkie stretched out his arm. "Grab my arm."

"You have wings, Butterfly. Believe in them!" Snow said.

Fly put her trust in Vulkie to carry them both. The wind against her ears chilled her new Bat body as she hung on to him.

"Let go," Vulkie suddenly said.

Fly looked up at him as her grip faltered, her claws sliding down to fit in his. She thought of Kiah's courage on the day he flew down to catch her. She thought of her own recklessness and what it had cost her in the service of the evil king. Every choice led to the moment of flight, of her own flight and her own doing. She was an Elf Bat. She had wings. Wings to carry her high.

"I got you, Fly. Let go now. Trust your wings."

Vulkie's words fell on deaf ears as Fly's heart beat louder than her breath and his voice. She only saw his mouth form the words as her head was tilted back to watch him.

"Let go," he said. "Just let go."

And she did.

SNOWBLIND

The Bat queen was flying. Snowblind circled about on the ground, eyes on the two Bats criss-crossing in the wild blue.

"What do I do with my arms?" Fly asked.

Soo chuckled. "Keep them at your sides or carry something with you if it makes you more comfortable."

"Just be natural, girl," Snowblind said. "Your wings are the size of a dragon's, and they will move with greater force than your arms and legs. You are meant to keep your limbs tight when you take off, and then you can maneuver your body however you want up in the air."

He assumed that Fly was no longer listening to his voice but continued to explain it to her. Elf Bat or not, the girl was full of energy and needed extra lessons in persistent timing and patience. "Think about where your wings go as you tumble in somersault or veer hard right or left. When you take off, hug your arms to your chest. Once you are up in the air, let your arms out against the wind. It is not natural for you, Fly. You are new to the world of flight."

"But she is one of us now," Soo said to him with confidence. "She's an Elf Bat."

"Not until the courage dive."

"What? Snow, she has just begun to balance in the sky."

"Tsunami," Snowblind said in a whisper, "time is short. When a baby Bat is born, they are born with wings attached.

Several years into childhood, each child must dive from the mother."

"Aye, Snow. I remember. But—"

"Tradition is our way." He pressed a claw hard against Soo's chest. "Fly must dive."

FLY

At Snow's order, Fly clumsily landed in the clearing to watch him shed his cloak and open his wings.

"Traditionally," he said, "it's the child's mother who brings the young Bat up. But I am eldest here so I will fill the role." He jerked his head over his shoulder. "Hop on. I'm taking you up."

"I won't hurt your back?"

"You will not. Come."

Fly swung one leg across his wings and her eyes widened when he suddenly shot up into the air.

"There will be no instinct for you," Snow said as he carried her through the clouds. "It is all an act of choosing to believe. Believe you have wings and they will catch you." He heard no response and shouted, "did you hear me, girl?"

"Aye," she said breathlessly.

"We are one mile up. Dive or I invert," he said. "Dive or I invert!"

At Fly's hesitation, he flipped upside down.

Kiah, Fly thought, *catch me.*

"Open your wings!"

"Catch her, Snow!"

"Fly, open your wings!"

She heard voices from the ground. All of them were calling to her.

The sensation of the wind whipping her hair and against her

chest.

Falling. She was tumbling through the air, spinning, out of control.

"Open your wings!"

Fly shrieked at the Bats on the ground, spreading her arms as she hurled down. *I have wings,* she told herself, *I am an Elf Bat.*

SNOWBLIND

Seconds before her body struck the ground, Fly flapped her Bat wings and catapulted back into the sky, flamboyantly twirling, wings wrapped around her small six-foot frame. And at the last moment, she tumbled down again, crashing in a heap into the trees.

"Well done, Butterfly," Snowblind said, landing sharply on the ground. "But if I may, much work is needed on your descent."

Fly rolled over, spitting out dirt.

"Timing is everything."

She snarled up at him, determination surging through every inch of her Bat body. Her brown and gold Bat eyes blinked as she surveyed the sky, pondering the next act for her wings. She had not noticed the change in her eye color, but Snowblind knew she could feel the difference. He began to share her mind, her thoughts, all of her senses. He knew she was gaining strength.

"The first taste of flight is all one needs to hunger for it again," he said.

Without further instruction, Fly flapped her wings and took to the sky, Vulkie and Fire flanking her. She crash-landed again, refusing to take Snowblind's claw. "Take me up for another dive."

"It is surging within you, isn't it? The Bat blood."

"I'll dive. Take me up again."

"Aye."

Snowblind flew up with her on his back, stopping at one mile. Fly dove without hesitation, dropping faster and faster, wings pressed tight into her body. She opened them three inches from the ground, landing with grace amongst the other Bats.

"That's great, Fly," Vulkie said, bounding eagerly beside her. "But you only know one trick. And your landings are sloppy."

At Fly's frustrated expression, he backed away with a mischievous smile. "Watch," he whispered. "Watch me."

Vulkie took flight and showed off his variety of advanced Bat stunts. Inverted flying, somersaults, lateral and back flips.

Fly's mouth gaped when she saw him manipulate clouds into new shapes using his wings.

"Childish antics," Snowblind said, looking up. "He can play in the sky, but he can't wield weapons in it."

"It looks so easy," Fly said.

"Ah. Because he was born with them. Becoming a Bat in the way that you have, Fly, is a challenge by itself. You aren't born knowing how to move so effortlessly."

"I'm here to learn, aren't I?"

"Indeed," Snowblind said. "If you can master a bow or blade in the clouds better than Vulkie, you are well beyond his skill in my book."

Vale folded his arms as he watched Vulkie in the air. He shot an amused look at Snowblind and chuckled. "He's happy because he found someone else who isn't battle-oriented and who just wants to play all day."

"Vulkie," Snow called out, "you have not come here to teach her games. This is war training. Be serious."

"Not until Kiah comes," Vulkie said from the sky.

"By the time Kiah returns, son, there will only be several hours between us and war. It will come quick."

FIRESTORM

In the meeting room, Firestorm filled nine cups with black coffee, speaking loudly as he poured. "I believe a proper toast is in order for our Butterfly. She has her claws, eyes, wings, and she astonished us all in her first flight."

They each grabbed a cup, holding them in the air and beaming at her. Snow stood apart, coffee in hand, face serious.

"Kiah will be proud of you, dearest," Soo said.

"How do you feel?" Tor asked.

Fly looked at the group of Bats, humbled at the attention. "I feel that I belong here. I feel like an Elf Bat."

Ty tilted his cup to his mouth. "You are," he said, and drank.

"Watching you in the air reminded me of my courage dive," Vale said. "I was so proud of myself when I heard my parents cheer for me. I didn't land perfectly on the first try, but I let instinct take care of me."

"How old were you on your first flight, Vale?" Fly asked him.

"I had just turned seven. A common age for the first dive."

"Have we not celebrated Fly enough today?" Snow suddenly slammed his empty cup onto the table. "This is a fight against Bloodmanghe. Playing about in the clouds is a waste of our time." He swiftly left the room, Fly staring after him.

"What's wrong with Master Snow?" she asked.

Tor laid a hand on her shoulder. "Don't mind him, beauty."

"He's thinking of his youngest daughter," Vulkie said softly. He traded looks with Firestorm who had also read Snow's thoughts as he had left the room.

Fly's shoulders drooped. "What was her name?"

"Meaghiea," the Bats said in unison.

FLY

On return to the library that night, Fly watched a sweaty Snow pace back and forth, glasses on his nose, book in hand, his gait weak. As he read aloud, his voice trembled. The wings at his back unfurled, taking up the entire width of the room.

"Is that a book of history, Master Snow?"

"It's poetry." He sounded out of breath. "My wife penned hundreds of writings in this book two years before she was killed on Banegildacht."

"Is any of it written in Bat language?"

"No. Descendant language." He refused to look at her.

"May I hear one of her poems?"

Snow turned two pages over and read from the text:

"Spirited wake, calamitous heart, ages and ages of sorrow.

Long missed, our lives bound, love written in scars,

Scars of even edge and depth.

Past stars and hills, rock and water, journey to you,

Back to you, forever home my love,

For every shriek and wing to the light of sky,

Forever home."

He took his glasses off. "My love wrote that for me on our wedding day."

"You had children?" Fly asked.

He closed his eyes. "Three daughters. All of them tortured to death by methods no living soul should imitate."

"My sorrow for you is not enough," Fly said. "But I am with sorrow. I carry it for you."

"There is no way to forgive such cruel actions. Sorrow does nothing for my pain."

"Your youngest," Fly said. "Meaghiea."

His eyes glistened at the name. "What about her?"

"How did they kill her?"

"Wings torn from her little body. They had hung her upside down from a branch. When I came running, I thought she was alive." He shuddered and closed his eyes. "She was only seven."

"There will be justice, Master Snow," Fly said. "We will fight together."

"She never got to do her courage dive."

"I will dive for her. For Meaghiea's honor."

"My girl," Snow said, touching a claw against her cheek, "you bear the same purity in your heart as she did. Same spirit. Same wonder." He bowed his head, touching his forehead to Fly's. "Do not lose that spark. Hear me? You are so much like my Meaghiea, Fly. Do not lose that spark."

Fly embraced Snow, emotion stirring between them as she realized how clearly he saw his daughters in her. The desire to protect her was the same desire he had on the night of Banegildacht. Fly felt this. Snow did not want to lose her. He had failed to defend once before. *Never again*, Fly told herself, *Snow won't see another precious female sacrificed.*

19

Arrow Rain

<u>FLY</u>

"Remember dueling Soo?" Caine asked Fly. "The same principles apply in the air."

"But he can't hear my footsteps."

"He can hear your wings. Dive, my love."

Fly tumbled down through the morning light, wings wrapped around her body as she veered right and opened them against the wind. Soo flew in behind her, striking the back of her legs with his claws and double-flipping to the ground.

"You must learn to dodge and deflect fire arrows. Control your body. Be in complete control, Fly," Snow called to her.

"In the chaos of battle, you will not always know which way is up," Soo said as he flew parallel to Fly. "The Bloodmanghe will target those who fly the fiercest. They will do everything to bring us down. You must sense the arrows at your back, dearest, as you won't always be staring them down from the air. Sense them and your wings will do the rest."

"Fire on my order!" Snow shouted.

Fly hovered, ears picking up the sounds of arrows being fitted to the bow. They would come from behind.

"Fire!"

Her wings sensed before she did, carrying her in a wild pattern around the sky as the Bats took their shots.

"Stay inverted," Snow said to her. "Hold it steady."

Fly remained upside down, allowing the power of her wings and the breath of the wind to stay her course amidst the arrow rain. With a glance up and to her left, she saw she was alone in the air.

"Pyro-cannon!" Vale called out.

She drew a piece from under her wings and threw it.

"No, Fly. Aim it at me. I can take it."

"Hush up, Ty," Vale said, and Fly giggled when she heard them start a banter and rumble on the grass below.

"I want to fly against all eight of you," she said. "Give everything you got."

Soo grinned, hearing Fly somersault overhead. "Did you hear that, Snow? She wants us to fire everything."

"So be it. Bats, aim your bows at our reckless queen."

The precision of Elf Bats was magic, Fly knew. They could not miss unless it was a failure with purpose. She remained in flight with her back to the eight, and in the seconds that she counted inside her head, the arrows flew up at once, bearing down less than inches from her limbs. But she maintained control, speed, and fluidity in the sky. She felt the strength of her wings, a magnificent strength, beyond what she had dreamed a Bat would be.

And she was one of them. She was their people. She belonged.

20

Kiah's Return

Kiah emerged from the forest, shielding his eyes from the glare of daylight. He stepped across the grass in cloak and black leather suit, king of the Bats, a renewed strength in his core. He looked up at the sky and saw three Bats flying. He recognized Vulkie and Fire by their pattern of flight. But the third Bat escaped his memory. He took off to meet them in the air, calling out to them.

"My brethren! Vulkie! Fire!"

They both turned, flapping their wings as they kept to the wind. They smiled at him and then at each other.

"And," Kiah paused, blue and purple streaked eyes following the inverted third Bat, "who is that?"

Vulkie winked. "You will know, my king."

The Bat righted itself and finally met Kiah's eyes.

"Fly," Kiah gasped.

"Kiah!"

Kiah dashed forward, wrapping his arms around her, their wings moving in unison. Fly shuddered in his embrace, tears welling in her eyes.

"You're home," she said, smiling as she stroked his hair. "I can feel your strength."

"The changes in your eyes, Fly. Your claws." Kiah cupped her chin. "My beautiful she-bat...I missed you so much."

SNOWBLIND

From the ground, looking up, Snowblind and Vale sensed the magic between the king and queen in the sky.

"I haven't seen a sight like that in a long time," Snowblind said.

"The unity flight. Always beautiful."

Kiah came down first, landing in a crouch, one knee grazing the ground. His brown hair fell into his eyes as he lifted his head. "Snow, I see you have taken good care of my Fly."

Snowblind bowed. "My king."

"Gather the others and come to the meeting room. We are soon to leave."

"Aye, Kiah."

FLY

The joy of Kiah's return was dimmed within the Sanctuary walls. The eight Bats knelt before him as he entered, cloak trailing behind him. Even the previously exuberant face of Vulkie was somber. Fly sensed, for the first time, the thoughts of everyone in the room. She was one with her Bats.

"Tell us the plan," Vale said. "We're ready."

"We attack at midnight."

Not a breath was heard.

"This midnight?" Ty asked.

"Aye." Kiah looked to Fly next to him, taking her claw in his, as he said, "follow me to my cave. All of you. Carry what you brought here."

Within the hour, they were gathered outside the walls of the Sanctuary and took to the sky, flying straight to Kiah's cave. No time was wasted in gathering pieces of armor, blades, and each Bat's stash of pyro-cannon. Fly lost track of Kiah when Fire drew her close to fit armor over her tunic. It did not feel as thick as what the Bloodmanghe would wear, having a more pliable hold against one's body.

"I don't need to layer so much," Fly said. "It will be too heavy to fly."

"Bats do not enter a fight without armor, little queen. The Bloodmanghe will aim to kill and you cannot risk a single hit to your heart."

Fly glanced at Vulkie, reading his mind as he thought of her unborn child. She gave a look toward Snow who stared at her from across the room. *They all know*, she thought.

"Do as we say, Fly," Vulkie said out loud. "For Kiah."

Fly nodded, then looked over her shoulder. "Where is Kiah?"

"He went upstairs."

She looked down at Fire who was securing leather braces around her legs. "The forbidden upstairs?"

"Aye. He never let you see it, did he?"

Fly saw Fire trade morose eyes with Vulkie. He looked back at her. "Go on. He needs you."

Tiny rocks crumbled around her feet as Fly went up the stairway. Her Bat senses created an ache in her chest as she ascended, slowing her before she reached the open room at the top. Her claws lightly scraped along the walls. The scent in the room was thick. A smell of death and pain. A smell of pure lavender, aged blood, and the musk of her beloved Kiah.

"She was right here. This is where she died."

Fly halted her step.

"They killed her. Right in front of me."

She knew Kiah sensed her presence, but he remained standing. He was staring at the back wall, shoulders hunched, glorious in full armor, but trembling in the way of a frightened child.

"Count Addis violated her. I saw nothing but her tortured face. And...the blade of the Bloodmanghe...cut her throat." His voice cracked as he dropped to his knees.

Fly knelt down behind him, wrapping her arms and wings around his shuddering body. She listened to him cry. Kiah leaned backward against her, collapsing into her embrace.

"I got you," Fly whispered. "I got you, Kiah." She closed her eyes and felt the song of Ialchagor flow through her lips. *K'adhlenalde*, she thought, *hear me.*

"Ialchagor," Kiah uttered. He sat up slowly, turning to face Fly. A small smile lit his fangs, and his eyes glistened. "You know Ialchagor."

Fly pressed her forehead to his, dark eyes downcast. "I sing for you. I sing for Kadhle."

"Pudding," Kiah said, lifting her chin with his claw, "thank you."

"I learned it for the Bats. For our people."

"Our people. Aye, my dear." He kissed her gently. "Your Bat eyes are magnificent."

"Come," Fly said. "Have your revenge."

21

War Cry

The Bats stood together in the hearth room, their sharp-colored eyes the sole source of light in the cave. Kiah and Fly came downstairs together, each casting a loving, protective gaze at their brethren who waited without a word.

"Three cups of strong coffee," Kiah said, gesturing to the ten cups set on the table, "is necessary on the hour before battle."

As each Bat took a cup and lifted it to their lips, they bowed their heads to Kiah and again to Fly. "Three cups of tea," Fire said with a smirk, "is a plea for coffee."

His joke failed to cheer the room, but Fly offered him a half-smile as he drank. They drank three cups each, their lips tight, eyes fierce, and hearts solemn.

"Tradition is a comfort," Kiah uttered. "To us all, it is a binding of wing and fang."

"We will follow you, my king," Snow said, dropping to one knee.

The other seven exchanged somber looks before following the act. Fly took Kiah's claw in hers and knelt before him, lifting her eyes to his.

"This is not a game of Bat tag. Nor is it a time for hiding in the shadow of rock and tree," Kiah said. "But I will not tell you how to fight. I know the pain you endure. I know the agony and grief. You may use whichever tactics you desire in attacking the counts, and you will destroy every anti-Bat possession in their homes."

The Bats nodded in unison.

"Each of you will approach the house of your count separately. Spindle will have two of his crew accompany you. Two crewmen for each Bat. Understood?"

"Aye, Kiah."

"Defend each other. Defend the skies."

"Females and children?" Tor asked.

"Keep them out of harm's way. Do what you must to protect the innocents. If any grown male purebreds attack, you have my permission to take them down. Aim your weapons at the counts and Bloodmanghe. They are the targets."

"Aye, Kiah. Understood."

"Fly and myself will be waiting at the top of the citadel until the horn blows within Adreachterum. Then we will go to Addis and the king. Vulkie, when I give my signal on the cliff, you and Fire stir the fog and mist cover. We will dive in formation off the top of Ialchagor."

At Kiah's silence, the eight Bats stood up and walked past him to fly out of the cave.

"Come," Kiah said to Fly.

Fly moved slow behind her husband as he exited their home. She looked around at what they were leaving behind. The rugged table and chairs, remnants of faded paintings, pages of ancient text of their people, and the safety of the cave. Kiah knew her fears and she knew his.

Come, my love, Kiah said in his mind.

The ten of them flew to the top of Ialchagor and perched on the edge. Kiah saw Fly studying each of her brethren, memorizing the colors of their eyes and outfits. Each Bat was dressed in a pale blue bodysuit, black cloak laid over layered leather armor, save for Kiah and Fly. The pair mirrored each other in white cloaks draped around their black suits and armor.

Kiah spoke into the night, pacing behind them. "They murdered our parents, grandparents, brothers, and sisters. They burned our books and heirlooms. They left us with nothing, and yet we were given life. For our blood, our kin, our honor, we avenge them all."

"Avenge Jekkiliah," Snowblind said, eyes locked on the dark horizon.

"Avenge Jekkiliah," the seven Bats repeated in unison.

"No fear," Kiah growled. "No hesitation. Make them remember us. They murdered our children. They took the lives of our females who carried unborn babes. Justice must come for them. It must come now."

"Avenge Jekkiliah," they said louder.

"The counts violated the bodies of our mothers. Our sisters." He looked sadly at Snowblind. "Our daughters."

FLY

Fly lifted her head to the stars, drawing in the crisp, clear air of the night. Soon there would be a fog laying thick to hide them. A shield to soar in. To avenge her people.

"Are you ready, pudding?"

Fly nodded, bowing her head to Kiah. He brought her chin back up. "Dive with me," he whispered. "Shriek into the night."

"Siobahorkeilde," Fly said softly.

"Shriek," Kiah breathed into her ear. "Let them hear you. Let them hear our queen."

The wings of each Bat unfurled behind them as they stiffened their shoulders, fixing their eyes on the city and outer villages below. Not one living soul would sleep tonight. All would be awoken.

"Banegildacht Siobahorkeilde!" Kiah screamed. He threw his head back, shaking out his hair, unclenching his claws. "Banegildacht Siobahorkeilde!"

The eight echoed him with primal shrieks in the night sky.

Banegildacht Siobahorkeilde.

Justice.

Honor.

Defending Home.

Fly lifted her head and hoarsely shrieked with her brethren. She opened her wings.

The time had come.

About the Author

Han M Greenbarg has been in love with writing fiction since childhood. She is an avid coffee drinker, proud dog mom, and lover of country music and war movies. Her biggest jolts of inspiration stem from nature, a variety of film scores, and animals of all kind.

You can connect with me on:

https://www.hanmgreenbarg.com

https://www.instagram.com/hanmgreenbargauthor

www.ingramcontent.com/pod-product-compliance
Lightning Source LLC
Chambersburg PA
CBHW031538310726
48971CB00008B/2536